Léon Bloy

.RANTULAS' PARLOR
THER UNKIND TALES

LÉON BLOY (1846-1917) was a French writer and journalist who was the author of essays, novels, short stories, as well as a diary in eight volumes. In 1867 he made the acquaintance of Jules-Amadée Barbey d'Aurevilly, who not only stoked up his literary ambitions but was also responsible for his conversion to ardent Catholicism. Although primarily remembered today for his journals and essays, his volume of short stories *Histoires désobligeantes* (of which the present volume is a translation) might well be his definitive work.

BRIAN STABLEFORD has been publishing fiction and non-fiction for fifty years. His fiction includes a series of "tales of the biotech revolution" and a series of metaphysical fantasies featuring Edgar Poe's Auguste Dupin. He is presently researching a history of French roman scientifique from 1700-1939 for Black Coat Press, translating much of the relevant material into English for the first time, and also translates material from the Decadent and Symbolist Movements.

Léon Bloy

The Tarantulas' Parlor

and Other Unkind Tales

Translated and with an Introduction by

Brian Stableford

THIS IS A SNUGGLY BOOK

ISBN: 978-1-943813-15-5

Contents

Introduction   *vii*

The Tisane   *3*
The Old Man of the House   *9*
Monsieur Pleur's Religion   *16*
The Tarantulas' Parlor   *26*
Plan for a Funeral Oration   *34*
The Captives of Longjumeau   *40*
A Bad Idea   *46*
Two Phantoms   *54*
The Terrible Punishment of a Dentist   *60*
Alain Chartier's Reawakening   *66*
The Obliging Stroker   *73*
The Monsieur's Past   *80*
"Whatever You Want!"   *88*
The Last Firing   *94*
The End of Don Juan   *100*
A Martyr   *106*
Suspicion   *113*
Calypso's Telephone   *119*
Worn Out   *124*
A Failed Sacrilege   *129*
"There's Trouble Brewing!"   *135*

The Silver Mote   *141*
A Well-Nourished Man   *146*
The Bean   *153*
Digestive Proposals   *159*
A Cry from the Depths   *166*
The Reading Room   *177*
No One's Perfect   *184*
"Let's Be Reasonable!"   *189*
Jocasta on the Sidewalk   *195*
Cain's Lucky Find   *202*
The Animal-Lover   *210*

Introduction

*H*ISTOIRES DÉSOBLIGEANTES by Léon Bloy, here translated as *The Tarantulas' Parlor and Other Unkind Tales*, was first published in Paris in 1894 by E. Dentu. The stories had previously been published in the pages of the literary periodical *Gil Blas* between July 1893 and April 1894. Although many secondary references in English transpose the title as "Disobliging Stories," I consider "Unkind Stories" to be more accurate as well as less clumsy.

Léon Bloy, the author of the *histoires désobligeantes*, was born in Périgueux in the Dordogne in 1846. He was the second of seven sons of a civil servant who had authoritarian tendencies and freethinking views, and a mother who was an "old-Fashioned Catholic." Initially, he followed his father's example, and when he was sent to Paris in 1864 to work for an architect he was attracted to radical socialism and fervent anticlericalism. He soon abandoned the job in which he had been placed, however, and enrolled in the École des Beaux-Arts in 1865. He also resumed the literary endeavors with which he had flirted in his teens, but could not publish any of the articles he wrote. In December 1867, however, his ideas and ambitions were transformed when he made the acquaintance of the man who lived on the opposite side of the corridor in the building where he was resident: the aging and eccentric writer Jules-Amadée Barbey d'Aurevilly. Barbey d'Aurevilly not only stoked up Bloy's literary ambitions but was responsible for his conversion to ardent Catholicism.

Like many sudden converts, Bloy immediately became very zealous in his new-found faith, and he managed to maintain that fervor at an exceptional intensity for an unusually long time. Although he was recovering his mother's faith, his zealotry remained indelibly stamped by Barbey d'Aurevilly's example. Barbey had also been raised as a freethinker and had converted at a considerably later age than his protégée, but had then become similarly zealous. His work as a literary critic, however, had given enthusiastic promotion to writers who were anything but Catholic in their outlook, including Honoré de Balzac and Gustave Flaubert, and his esthetic allegiances never wavered in the light of his renewed faith—although it certainly colored his view of the writers he admired; he famously remarked that another of his favorites, Charles Baudelaire, was so convinced in his Satanism that he had no possible destiny but suicide or "the foot of the cross." Barbey's own literary work had followed very conspicuously in radical Romantic footsteps, and his late-found Catholicism served to give him a particular interest in penetrating the depths of the human soul in search of the authentic roots of original sin—which, of course, he had no difficulty in convincing himself that he had found, in all their mandragoric horror.

Léon Bloy, who had to get used to being thought of and described as Barbey's first and last disciple, inevitably followed a similar trajectory. His literary ambitions had to be shelved for a while, however, when he was conscripted for military service during the Franco-Prussian War of 1870, and was not able to return to Paris until 1873. Barbey then assisted him to write for the Catholic periodical *L'Univers*, edited by the famous Catholic polemicist Louis Veuillot, but Veuillot found Bloy too flamboyant in both his style and his thinking, and the relationship was short-lived. Bloy began to form literary friendships, but had a tendency to alienate those of his friends who were not devout by virtue of his strenuous attempts to convert them. Jean Richepin and Paul Bourget both found him inconvenient in that respect, although he formed a more stable bond with another aging Catholic writer, Ernest Hello. He did one or two odd jobs in order to earn money, but could not settle to any kind of regular work.

In 1877 Bloy began a passionate affair with a part-time prostitute, Anne-Marie Roulé, whose conversion was operated more smoothly than others he had attempted, and the two of them entered into a kind of mystical and visionary "adventure," assisted by Hello, which some might have regarded as a *folie à deux*, although Anne-Marie was the only one who ended up committed to a lunatic asylum, in 1882. Bloy returned more wholeheartedly to the literary community when his cousin, Émile Goudeau, the founder of the famous literary club of the Hydropathes, introduced him to Le Chat Noir, the café where the Hydropathes had partially reformed. Richepin was a regular there, as were Alphonse Allais and Edmond Haraucourt. It was shortly thereafter that Bloy met Villiers de l'Isle Adam, with whom he formed a fast friendship, soon to become a threesome, to which he referred as the "Concile de Gueux" [Synod of Vagabonds], by virtue of the addition of Joris-Karl

Huysmans. Bloy fell out with Goudeau and was soon *persona non grata* at Le Chat Noir, but by 1884, he was beginning to publish his work, and had started work on what were eventually to become his two published novels.

In 1886 Bloy finished *Le Désesperé* [The Desperate Man] an autobiographical novel, but the intended publisher backed out of issuing it for fear of prosecution, and it had to be diverted to a less timorous outlet for publication in 1887. In 1886 he had a brief liaison with Henriette Maillet, who was subsequently to serve as the model for Madame Chantelouve in Huysmans' classic account of Parisian Satanism *Là-Bas* (1891)—the first of a series of relationships he had with women of dubious reputation, one of whom bore him a son in 1888. There were no such problems with Jeanne Molbech, however, whom he married in 1890—although several of their mutual acquaintances are said to have tried to dissuade her from marrying him because of his dubious reputation.

Both Barbey-d'Aurevilly and Villiers de l'Isle Adam died in 1889, taking away two of Bloy's closest friends; Ernest Hello had died in 1885. Bloy and Joris-Karl Huysmans had already quarreled by the time Bloy published an article on *Là-Bas* that removed any hope of reconciliation, and after 1891 Bloy must have felt increasingly isolated outside of his marriage. On the other hand, his adventures in journalism were becoming increasingly successful by then; he had begun publishing in *Gil Blas* in 1888 and had then became a regular contributor to *La Plume* in 1890—but his often-scathing commentaries not only lost him more friends but won him some serious enemies. In 1892 he published his first article in the *Mercure de France*, which was eventually to become his principal outlet.

Bloy's relationship with *Gil Blas* reached its peak while the series of *Histoires désobligeantes* were appearing there in 1893-4; he did a great deal of work for the magazine, and although he was at odds with some of the editorial staff and always bitter about the low rates of pay he was receiving, it was the closest thing to a stable income he had ever had—very useful given that he had a wife and two children to support. Alas, it all went horribly wrong. By this time, the only close friend he had left was the Belgian painter Henry de Groux, but he was still prepared to leap to the defense of others he thought unjustly attacked, and when the anarchist sympathizer and Symbolist poet Laurent Tailhade was injured in a bomb blast, occasioning comments from journalists hostile to his politics who suggested that it was a kind of poetic justice, Bloy was outraged. He wrote a scathing demolition of the most outspoken sniper, Edmond Pelletier, which appeared in *Gil Blas* in April 1894.

Unfortunately Pelletier took the insult to heart and immediately called Bloy out—but Bloy thought that dueling was a stupid and barbaric custom and he refused to fight. Unfortunately, Jules Guérin, *Gil Blas'* editor, then felt obliged to accept the challenge in his stead, and was wounded in the contest. Holding Bloy responsible for the entire fiasco, Guérin immediately banished him from the pages of *Gil Blas* forever, bringing the series of "unkind tales" to an abrupt but faintly ironic conclusion. Bloy never returned to that kind of enterprise.

To say that Bloy was a difficult man to get along with would probably be a gross understatement, but a spiky personality and a tendency to get carried away by passion can be a considerable assistance to a writer's verve and expressive ability. It is also worth noting that he was often as hard on himself as he was on others, and was under no illusions about his own failings. If some of the *histoires désobligeantes* contain veiled cruelties addressed to his ex-friends, some of them also contain scantily-clad cruelties addressed to himself, which add to the fulminatory sarcasm that is their most interesting and idiosyncratic quality. Thus, for instance, it useful to bear in mind, when considering a story like "Cain's Lucky Find," that it is not the story's notional narrator but the object of the narrator's savage bile that is a disguised portrait of the author. Bloy was just as likely to consider himself, literally and symbolically, as a fantasist, a fool and a failure as he was to hurl such accusations at others, and that tendency makes it unsurprising that he considered, with every justification, the self-reflective "The Silver Mote" to be his own favorite among his works. It was the kind of story that he could always look back on with satisfaction, as a story so typical of his endeavors that no one else was likely to have written it—which is exactly the kind of reward that true writers seek.

Because of this marked trait of self-dissatisfaction, emphasized rather than undermined by his assertive arrogance and explosive bile, Bloy was, and remains, a more complex and profound individual and writer than his reputation suggests. Thus, in the story that I have selected as a title-piece for the collection—because it is a more distinctive and dramatic label than any simple translation of the original could be—the author is not taking a position in the shoes of the "fly" introduced into the "spider's parlor" in order to offer a straightforward study in contemptuous absurdity, but rather taking an imaginative sidestep in order to look at some of his own sinful tendencies, and to consider a fate that might conceivably, admittedly in grotesque circumstances, have been his own. It is as well, in reading many of these stories, to remember that the actual location of an author's eyesight is not necessarily in the ocular apparatus of the ostensible viewpoint character, and that much of a story's force, as well as its distinctiveness, can derive from some such displacement.

The controversy constantly whipped up by Bloy's antics and endeavors undoubtedly assisted his public profile, and probably lent impetus to his career, but it must have been discomfiting nevertheless; the status of ultimate *enfant terrible* is hardly an easy one to wear, even in a city as proudly fond of its *enfants terribles* as Paris. It was probably inevitable that Bloy would become and remain much more prolific as a journalist than as a novelist, producing combative essays a-plenty over a wide spectrum of subjects, but it was less expectable that he would owe his ultimate fame to his journals and letters, becoming more of a specimen than an artist. That was presumably a far cry from his initial ambition, but it remains the case that the two novels and two volumes of short stories that he produced are themselves primarily interesting as specimens, if not of literal autobiography then at least of the strange working of a highly idiosyncratic mind.

The ultimate shape of his oeuvre testifies very obviously to the fact that Bloy had great difficulty focusing his effort on literary objectives demanding time and extensive shaping, except perhaps when he was developing his religious ideas. As the two extracts that the author included in the series of *Histoires désobligeantes* clearly illustrate, his second novel, *La Femme pauvre* [The Poor Woman] (1897) was a patchwork affair written in fits and starts, and it is not surprising that he never completed—or even seriously attempted—a third. Short stories, however, were more his cup of tea, the present exemplar following swiftly on the heels of *Sueur de Sang* [Blood-Sweat] (1894), which is mostly based on his experiences as a conscript during and after the Franco-Prussian War, and there is considerable cause for regret in the fact that he was not able to continue the series of *Histoires désobligeantes*, or supplement it with a third series.

It was, in fact, while Bloy was writing his short story series that he resumed his journal—which had also been a patchwork affair of fits and starts before then—in real earnest, and it is probable that the discipline of writing the regular story series assisted him to cultivate the discipline of keeping his journal, and helped paved the way for his virtual abandonment of fiction once he began publishing his autobiographical commentary in *Le Mendiant ingrate* [The Ungrateful Beggar] (1898)—the first of a sequence that eventually stretched to a series of eight volumes. Several samplers of his correspondence have also been published, mostly posthumously, and are still serving to maintain a trickle of "original" work today, long after his death in 1917.

As is well-known, however, there are lies, damn lies, statistics and autobiography, and while truth is sometimes stranger than fiction, fiction is always truer, so it is probably a mistake to look for the real Léon Bloy in his non-fictional writing, especially his journals. The real man is only contained in his fiction—and, because of the very particular and peculiar kind of fiction it is, the truest reality is to be found in his short fiction, simply because that is its most paradoxical location. Given the unusual kind of man he was, as well as the historical interval in which he was writing fiction most prolifically, it was natural that he should become an exponent of a very distinctive subgenre of fiction, and find a natural home for it in the briefly-hospitable pages of *Gil Blas*. It was natural too that he should begin to use his regular slot there to dabble in the genre of the *conte cruel*, which has a fascinating history of its own.

※

Gil Blas was one of the first literary periodicals to make extensive use in its pages of short fiction adapted to a length that had long been standardized as the "normal" length of an episode of a newspaper feuilleton serial, which was between 1,400 and 1,800 words. In the past, most weekly and monthly periodicals, and even daily ones, had favored more substantial short stories, because there was no convenient narrative technique for reducing stories to the conventional length of a *feuilleton* episode. The rapid proliferation of Parisian periodicals in the 1880s, however, assisted by new technologies of paper production and printing, encouraged experimentation, and several periodicals began to play host to that "streamlined" format, which was picked up from *Gil Blas* by two of the leading Parisian daily newspapers, *Le Journal* and *Le Matin*. Both papers continued to run feuilleton serials—indeed, *Le Matin* had the most successful *feuilletonist* of the period on its staff in Gaston Leroux—but when *Le Journal* began focusing more intently on short fiction, *Le Matin*'s editor soon introduced a new occasional feature, *Le Mille-et-un Matins*, intensifying competition in that curious corner of the marketplace.

The modification of literary technique required to produce short stories in that narrow length-format inevitably encouraged various strategies of abbreviation, which cut out much of the methodical introduction and explanatory exposition previously typical of story-construction, but it also required a new approach to the subject-matter of stories. Edgar Allan Poe had pointed out in the 1840s that, simply because short stories *are* short, they have to focus more intently on their endings than longer ones, and on the quickest way of getting there. Longer stories, by definition, take the scenic route, and the longer they are, the more important the route becomes by comparison with the destination. There is, therefore, a sense in which novels can, and do, have very similar endings, expending most, if not all, of their artistry in arriving there by different routes—it was a cliché even in the nineteenth century to observe that most novels ended with a marriage and an inheritance—while short stories, especially very short stories, are greatly encouraged, if not actually compelled by the logic of their different aspiration, to use similar methods to arrive at destinations which seem in some way out of the ordinary.

In the days when short stories had not yet fully embraced that quest for novelty, and still frequently aimed for the same clichés as longer ones—marriage, enrichment and the frustration of villainy—those endings had often been called "morals," because their qualification as endings was based on their affirmation of moral principles: an affirmation seen by many readers and critics as an essential function of story-telling, and of art in general. Writers in search of realism, however—a much larger minority within their category than that of readers in search of realism comprise in theirs—had often been rather resentful of the expectations imposed by "morals" of this sort, which clearly do not reflect the world as it is. A genre of short fiction had thus grown up whose initial designation, in the classic collection *Champavert* (1831) by "Petrus Borel le lycanthrope," was *contes immoraux*: "immoral" tales. That designation was essentially sarcastic, because it was underlain by the tacit contention that "morals" are not moral at all, because they are lies, and that only "immoral tales" can be truly moral, by virtue of being truthful, accurately reflecting the horrid immortality of the world as it really is.

Obviously, writers were able to see from the outset that endings deliberately defying conventional expectations of how stories "ought" to end offered much more scope for variation and originality, as well as accuracy, than stories that simply endorsed conventional expectations. They were also able to see from the outset—and if they were in any doubt, the fate of Petrus Borel le lycanthrope would have provided a striking exemplar—that, if they elected to follow that literary route, they would be setting themselves against the current of reader demand. While the cowards among them decided that it was, on the whole, safer not to do that, the arrogant, the perverse and the heroic (the three categories are not necessarily identical) boldly set off on a difficult crusade, at least to challenge, if not to change, the apparent pattern of reader demand. It was a crusade that they did not win, perhaps inevitably, but it was one in which there was always some slight hope of establishing at least a fugitive kingdom in Jerusalem.

A new label for what such rebel short-story writers were doing was provided by another classic collection of "anti-moral" short stories, the Comte de Villiers de l'Isle-Adam's *Contes cruels* (1883). That label stuck, although the equivalent suggested by the first English translation of that collection, *Sardonic Tales*, failed to do so, and English critics have mostly had to be content with the French label—of which they had far less necessity, English writers being, for the most part and well into the twentieth century, not much given to heroic perversity, mostly choosing to manifest their arrogance in other ways. Precisely because the label had been used as a title, however, many other French writers were reluctant simply to adopt it, and tended to avoid it. Two of the leading successors of Villiers, who, between them, did more than anyone else to formulate "production-lines" of such stories, Guy de Maupassant and Octave Mirbeau, forsook category description altogether, and their example was followed by Catulle Mendès, Jean Lorrain and many other writers whose short work was only described as *contes cruels* by critics. Others, however, tried out variants; Jean Richepin subtitled two his collections of tales from *Gil Blas* and *Le Journal* "*histoires horribles*" [horrible stories] and "*contes sans morale*" [stories without morals], while Léon Bloy preferred *Histoires désobligeants*.

It should not be thought that in substituting "*désobligeante*" for "*cruel*," Bloy intended to signify that his stories were somehow milder than Villiers'. Although Bloy was notorious for being a fervent and arrogant Catholic, whereas Villiers had been much weaker in his attempts to muster religious faith and render it conspicuous, that certainly did not make Bloy any less cruel in his judgments of his fellow men, or of himself. Quite the reverse, in fact; bigotry and repentance are more prolific sources of cruelty than faithlessness, and have the added twist of a hypocrisy that encourages them to boast of their compassion when their cruelty is at its most vicious. Only someone sincerely and heroically prepared to believe the inconceivable can maintain a straight face when saying that it is sometimes necessary to be cruel in order to be kind—or, in Bloy's terms, unkind in order to be obliging.

Villiers de l'Isle Adam, who was sometimes in danger of starving to death, had been driven to literary mass-production in the 1880s by the fact that he had a son to protect, and he joined in with the new glut of *contes cruels* prompted by the lead given by *Gil Blas* to other fashion-conscious periodicals. He called one of his new collections *Nouveaux contes cruels* (1888) but even he felt the need to find alternatives, and floundered somewhat in that quest, only being able to come up with *Histoires insolites* (1888), which translates as "unusual" or "eccentric" stories. His death in 1889, however, prevented him from cashing in on the boom that followed when *Le Journal* expanded the marketplace dramatically in the 1890s, and by the time that Léon Bloy joined the game in earnest, his chief competition was provided by Maupassant, Richepin and Mirbeau.

The logic of the situation ensured that there really was a competition, not so much in the vulgar sense that Bloy was competing with other writers for the regular "*conte cruel* slot" in the pages of *Gil Blas* as in the sense that the quest for originality forced by the new convention of defying the old conventions put a rather different burden on creativity, and that once a particular cruelty had been devised, it could not be enough merely to imitate it. Although it is not true of marriages, as Leo Tolstoy once pretended, there is an obvious sense in which all happy endings are alike, while every unhappy one has to be unhappy in its own way. The fashionability of *contes cruels* brought about by the fashionability of ultra-short stories moved the goalposts of literary creativity not merely toward "anti-moral" endings but toward endings that had to strive for originality in their "anti-morality"

It is probably an advantage to remember, in reading these stories today, that they were produced in a phase of literary evolution that was exploratory and experimental, and hence intrinsically exciting. That experimental and exploratory phase did not last long; like virtually all the other literary fashions of *fin-de-siècle* Paris, it began to fade away after the turn of the century, into decadence if not to disrepute. The lessons learned as a result of the experimentation became standardized themselves; they became aspects of stories that were slick, smart and sophisticated, rather than arrogant, perverse and heroic, and were modified by sufficient blandness to make them amenable to authentic mass-production, and hence for use in America, where a measure of literary-moral hypocrisy remained inviolable for decades to come. What Léon Bloy was doing in his "unkind tales" was, however, new, not merely to him but in a general sense. Borel and Villiers had erected key signposts, but the terrain was still largely unexplored, and the wilderness was vast enough to accommodate numerous explorers working in different directions with slightly different equipment.

It is probably also helpful to remember that the development and evolution of the *conte cruel* was not independent of the other literary movements that provided its historical context and cultural environment—far from it, in fact. There were two major literary Movements in full swing in the 1890s whose apparent competition—far more apparent than real—provided a basic thesis and antithesis for writers in search of a fundamental philosophy and methodology: Naturalism and Symbolism. Both movements, but particularly the latter, were entangled with the parallel "Decadent Movement." The origins and evolution of each of these three terms had been complex, generated by a series of disputes and arguments that had as much accident as logic about them, and all three are more easily characterized by what they were supposedly against rather than what they were supposedly striving to achieve, but they nevertheless provided the ideas that dominated authorial thought in *fin-de-siècle* Paris.

In crude terms, Symbolists, especially those prepared to consider themselves as exponents of "decadent style," favored ornate language, impressionistic language and indirect expression of meaning, tacitly figuring that one could get a better imaginative grip on reality by looking at it askance, and a trifle vaguely. Naturalists, on the other hand, were more concerned with psychological and sociological analysis of the manner in which social relationships work, and tended to favor a literary gaze that was not merely direct but intense and penetrative. Although many Naturalists thought that the ornate, impressionistic and indirect expression of the Decadent style got in the way of what they were trying to do, revelation of the "moral decadence" of contemporary society and its members was a key element of their program, and the affiliates of the Decadent Movement routinely conflated the two senses of the term "decadent" in such a way as to make their own attitude seem hybrid, although the critical predominance of the former meaning often led to their simply being lumped in with the Symbolists. Because their basic literary orientations were different, however, there was nothing to prevent Naturalists from using Symbolist devices, and nothing to inhibit Symbolists from aspiring to a kind of "naturalism" of their own, especially in terms of moral perspective.

Many writers, therefore, moved between the two major movements, sometimes seemingly changing their allegiance—like Joris-Karl Huysmans, who started out as a Naturalist by conviction and reputation but then became one of the key central exemplars of the Decadent Movement—but more often simply refusing to be tied down either methodically or in terms of reputation, to the extent that they could evade that bondage. The most arrogant always considered themselves above such things as "movements," wanting both not merely to be but to be universally considered *sui generis*. Léon Bloy was of that number, perhaps less convincingly than Guy de Maupassant or Jean Richepin, but no less determinedly. Perhaps more significantly, however, the entire subgenre of *contes cruels* was necessarily hybridized. By virtue of its shortness, especially in exemplars aiming at the ultra-shortness promoted by *Gil Blas* and *Le Journal*, it had to employ impressionistic techniques of description, substituting swift symbolism for explanatory exposition, and it had to rely very heavily on attempted, or at least pretended, psychological and sociological analysis, and the potential of such analysis to lay hypocrisy bare, in order to provide suitably cruel endings.

It might seem paradoxical that ornate language, which gives an impression of prolixity, can be very useful in the construction of short stories, but as Edgar Allan Poe had demonstrated—a demonstration that had been taken to heart by his many French admirers, and had contributed considerably to his remarkable dearth of American admirers—ornate language can actually be very economical, precisely because it is so impressionistic and unpedestrian. That fact, and consciousness of it, lay behind that elaborate development in France of the format of the prose-poem, which provided important exemplars for the development of the *conte cruel* in the work of Charles Baudelaire.

The fact that Léon Bloy uses ornate language very frequently as a narrative device probably reflects the fact that a lot of the other writers with whom he socialized were at the core of the Symbolist Movement—as is evident in the dedications that he religiously attached to his works—and it certainly contributes greatly to the temptation to regard him as a significant exponent of Decadent style. His own purpose, however, was not to seek any such affiliation to that kind of literary cause, but always to search for a particular naturalism of his own—a naturalism which, not in spite of but because of its cruelty and its infusion with religious conviction, was markedly different in stripe from the Naturalism of Émile Zola. It is worth noting that *Gil Blas*, although shunning any formal affiliation, leaned more to Naturalism than Symbolism—it serialized several of Zola's key works as well as helping to promote the career of Paul Bourget, who became the key exemplar of "neo-Naturalism" when Zola's star began to fade—and tended to honor ornate language more as an exercise in grotesquerie than symbolism. Bloy's reign as one of the masters of the periodical's *conte cruel* slot might have been rudely cut short, but one wonders how long, in any case, he could have kept up the sustained frenzy that their regular production required.

Within the entire canon of the *conte cruel*, Bloy has not generally been regarded as a leading player. His work in that vein is certainly not as deft as that of such contemporaries as Maupassant and Mirbeau, although it stands up reasonably well in comparison to Villiers' later work, but it is worth remembering that he only occasionally aspired to literary dexterity, and was always more interested in trying out new and potentially-interesting ways to work the oracle. He was very conscious of the fact that he was working in a relatively new arena, where many matters of technique had yet to be tried; some of those he attempted might now be judged wanting, but that does not reflect badly on his ambition, and much of what he achieved was not only genuinely unsettling in the mid-1890s but is still intriguingly unusual today.

By modern standards, Bloy's "punch-lines" often seem to be conspicuously "telegraphed," sometimes even by his titles, but he was never a manufacturer of surprises, always more interested in bitter confirmation than wry wrong-footing, and if his conscious intentions sometimes went awry, that is at least partly compensated by the fact that his anecdotal poses often cast their narrators as well as their targets in a very unkindly light. That aspect of his work retains a distinctiveness that makes it precious; in striving to discover and fabricate originality, Léon Bloy sometimes succeeded in being genuinely original—an achievement that is considerably rarer than one might imagine. That fact alone makes this translation of his work long overdue.

※

This translation has been made from the version of the first edition reproduced in the Bibliothèque Nationale's website *gallica*. The author's fondness for eccentric and esoteric expressions has inevitably caused some difficulties, and his sometimes-elaborate wordplay occasionally resists translation entirely, but I have reproduced his style—including its deliberate eccentricity and esotericism—as accurately as I could, keeping the use of explanatory footnotes to what seemed to me to be a reasonable minimum.

At the time of writing there is no searchable version of *Gil Blas* available on-line, so I have not been able to ascertain the original publication dates of all the stories, but the items from the first half of the collection are reproduced on a website entitled *Le Rayon Littéraire*, and I have recovered some bibliographical data from there, which is included in the footnotes.

Brian Stableford

THE TARANTULAS' PARLOR

AND OTHER UNKIND TALES

The Tisane

To Henry de Groux[1]

J ACQUES thought that it was simply ignoble of him. It was odious to stay there, in the dark, like a sacrilegious spy, while that woman, utterly unknown to him, made her confession.

But then, it would have been necessary for him to leave right away, as soon as the priest in the surplice had arrived with her, or, at least, to make a little noise in order that they might be alerted to the presence of a stranger. It was too late now, and the horrible indiscretion could only be further aggravated.

At a loose end, seeking, as woodlice do, a cool place at the end of the scorching day, he had taken it into is head, by no means in conformity with his usual whims, to

---

1 Henry de Groux (1866-1930) was a Belgian painter and sculptor affiliated to the Symbolist school whose other members included Fernand Khnopff and Jean Delville. He moved to Paris in the late 1880s, and his journal is a significant document of the Parisian artistic community in that era. He was Bloy's closest friend while the story series was in progress, and it is hardly surprising that his name crops up elsewhere in the collection. "La Tisane" was originally published in the 22 juillet 1893 issue of *Gil Blas*.

come into the old church and sit in the dark corner behind the confessional, in order to daydream while watching the great rose-window darken.

After a few minutes, without knowing how or why, he had become the involuntary witness of a confession.

It is true that the words did not reach him distinctly, and that, in sum, he could only hear a whisper—but the conversation seemed to become more animated toward the end. A few syllables, here and there, stood out, emerging from the opaque flow of that penitential chatter, and the young man—who, miraculously, was the very opposite of a perfect boor—simply dreaded overhearing confessions that were evidently not intended for him.

Suddenly, that possibility as realized. A violent stir seemed to occur. The immobile waves groaned as they split, as if to let some monster surge forth, and the listener, crushed by fear, heard these words proffered impatiently:

"I tell you, Father, that I've put poison in his tisane!"

Then nothing. The woman whose face was invisible got up from the prie-Dieu and silently disappeared into the thicket of darkness.

As for the priest, he made no more movement than a dead man, and slow minutes went by before he opened the door and came out in his turn, with the heavy step of a man stunned.

It required the persistent carillon of the beadle's keys and the injunction to leave to be repeated several times in the nave for Jacques to get up himself, so astounded was he by that statement, which was resounding within him clamorously.

He had recognized his own mother's voice!

4

Oh, he could not possibly be mistaken. He had even recognized her gait when the shadow of the woman had loomed up two paces away from him.

But then, what! Everything crumbled, everything fled, everything was nothing but a monstrous joke!

He lived alone with his mother, who rarely saw anyone else and only went out to go to mass. He was accustomed to venerating her with all his heart, as a unique exemplar of righteousness and generosity.

As far as he could see into the past, there was no disturbance, no obliquity, no secrecy, not a single deviation. A beautiful white road, as far as the eye could see, beneath a pale sky—for the poor woman's existence had been very melancholy.

Since the death of her husband, killed at Champigny,[1] whom the young man scarcely remembered, she had not ceased to wear mourning, occupying herself exclusively with the education of her son, whom she had not left for a single day. She had never wanted to send him to school, fearing the contacts he might make, and had taken complete charge of his instruction, building his soul with morsels of her own. He had even retained from that regime an anxious sensitivity, and singularly vibrant nerves, which exposed him to ridiculous pains, and perhaps also to veritable dangers.

When adolescence had arrived, the anticipated escapades that she had been unable to prevent had made her a little sadder, without affecting her gentleness. No

---

1 Champigny was within the location of the most significant attempt by French troops to break the Prussian siege of Paris in November 1870, more commonly known as the Battle of Villiers. The French suffered a catastrophic defeat and lost some 9,000 troops.

reproaches or mute scenes. She had, like so many others, accepted that which is inevitable.

In any case, everyone spoke about her with respect, and he alone, her very dear son, now found himself bound to disapprove of her—to disapprove of her on his knees, with tears in his eyes, as the angels might disapprove of God if he did not keep his promises!

Truly, it was enough to drive someone mad, to make one howl in the street. His mother! A poisoner! It was insane, a million times absurd; it was absolutely impossible—and yet, it was certain. Had she not just declared it herself? He could have torn his hair out.

But whom had she poisoned? Good God! He did not know of anyone in the neighborhood who had been poisoned. It was not his father, who had received a volley of grapeshot in the gut. It was not him, either, that she might have tried to kill. He had never been ill, never had need of a tisane, and knew that he was adored. The first time he had been late home, and that was certainly not for good reasons, she had been ill with anxiety herself.

Was it something that had happened prior to his birth? Her father had married her for her beauty, when she was scarcely twenty years old. Had that marriage been preceded by some adventure that might have involved a crime?

No, though. That limpid past was familiar to him; he had been told about it a hundred times over, and the evidence was too certain.

Why, then, that terrible confession?

Above all, why, oh why, had he overheard it?

Drunk with horror and despair, he went home.

His mother immediately ran to kiss him.

"How late you are, my dear child! And how pale you are! Are you ill?"

"No," he replied, "I'm not ill, but this intense heat is tiring, and I don't think I'll be able to eat anything. What about you, Mother? Aren't you feeling ill? You've been out, doubtless to get a breath of fresh air? I thought I saw you from a distance on the quay."

"I did go out, but you couldn't have seen me on the quay. I've been to confession—which I believe you haven't done for a long time, you bad boy."

Jacques was astonished that he did not choke, did not fall over, thunderstruck, as often happened in the novels he had read.

It was true, then, that she had been to confession! He had not fallen asleep in the church, and that abominable catastrophe had not been a nightmare, as he had momentarily imagined, crazily.

He did not fall, but he became much paler, and his mother was alarmed by that.

"What's the matter, then, my little Jacques?" she said. "You're suffering, and you're hiding something from your mother. You ought to have more confidence is the woman who loves only you, and has no one but you in all the world. How you're looking at me! My dear treasure . . . but what's the matter, then? You're scaring me."

She took him in her arms, lovingly.

"Listen to me, big baby. I'm not inquisitive, as you know, and I don't want to judge you. Don't tell me anything, if you don't want to tell me anything, but let me take care of you. You're going to be all right. In the meantime, I'll make you a nice little meal, which I'll bring you myself, won't I? And if you have a fever tonight, I'll make you a tisane. . . ."

This time, Jacques did fall down.

"Finally!" she sighed, a trifle wearily, reaching out for the bell-cord.

Jacques had an aneurism in its critical phase, and his mother had a lover who did not want to be a stepfather.

This simple drama took place three years ago in the vicinity of Saint-Germain-des-Prés. The house that was its theater belongs to a demolition specialist.

The Old Man of the House

To Charles Cain[1]

"OH, she can commend herself for having virtue, Madame Alexandre! Can you imagine! For three years she's supported him, that old crook, that old swindler—you can be sure that if he wasn't her father she'd have given him his marching orders a long time ago, to send him to the public hospice. But what can you do? You have to keep up appearances, to subsidize your parents if you don't have children or a dog, especially when you're in commerce. Oh, the family! Calamity after calamity! And there are those who say that there's a good God! The camel's back is going to break one of these fine mornings, isn't it?"

The extreme frequency of this filial monologue had unfortunately reduced its freshness. Not a day passed when Madame Alexandre did not complain in those terms about the harshness of her destiny.

Sometimes, however, she softened, when it was necessary for her to pour out her heart to one of her young

---

1 Charles Cain was an artist and engraver whose 1870 portrait of Bloy had been used as a frontispiece in the author's first collection, *Sueur du sang*. "Le Vieux de la maison" first appeared in the 29 juillet 1893 issue of Gil Blas.

clients who had not quite grasped the nobility of her jeremiads.

"Dear old Papa," she cooed, then, "if you only knew how much we love him. We only have a heart in order to cherish him. The trade has nothing to do with it, you see. We might be lowly placed in the world, be wretched, if you like, but the heart still speaks. One remembers one's childhood, the pure joys of the family, and I feel elevated in my own eyes, I swear, when I see that venerable old man crowned with white hair, who makes us think of the celestial fatherland, coming and going about the house."

Etc., etc.

Professional unconsciousness doubtless permitted the old shrew to take up, with equal good faith, either position—and the septuagenarian guest, alternatively dressed in glory and ignominy, squatted in his daughter's house, number 12, in the unalterable serenity of the evening of his life, like a hospital wreck on the bank of the great collector.

To tell the truth, the story of those two individuals had none of the essential qualities that one demands of an epic poem.

Ferdinand Bouton, commonly known as Papa Ferdinand or "the Old Man," was an old rogue from the Rue de Flandres, where he had once followed thirty professions, the least inadmissible of which had put his liberty in danger several times.

Mademoiselle Léontine Bouton, who was to be Madame Alexandre one day, and whose mother had disappeared shortly after her birth, had been brought up by the worthy man in the most rigorous principles of dishonesty. Prepared, from a very tender age, for humble work, she had hooked, at thirteen, a brilliant situation as an oblate virgin in the home of a Genevan millionaire renowned for his virtue, who called her his "angel of light" and completed her putrefaction. Two years sufficed for the debutant to wear out that Calvinist.

After that how many others! Recommended, above all, to discreet gentlemen, she became something like an employment agency for fathers, and progressed, until the age of eighteen, in an aureole of turpitude.

At that time, having become serious herself, by dint of rubbing up against serious people, she lost contact with her father, whose crapulous drunken frivolity, having become excessive, made her sick.

Fifteen years had passed during which the abandoned individual had had his fill of misfortune. Having lost the habit of business, unable to recover his old shrewdness, he was like an old fly that no longer has the strength to fly to excrement, and whom even spiders would no longer want.

Léontine, more fortunate, had prospered. Without raising herself to the top rank of public Gallantry, for whose mastery her incorrigible boorish manners did not permit her to yearn, she was able to maneuver in subaltern employments with so much artistry and obliging ambidextrousness that she insinuated herself, installed herself and wedged herself firmly into the hearty revelries, never forgetting to fill her glass before the bottle had completed the round. She was so spiteful before God and men, that she was able to defy misfortune.

Misfortune then arrived, in the grotesque and phantasmal form of her father.

The old clown, just as he was about to sink forever into the most unfathomable gulf, had found out that his daughter, his Titine, almost famous now under the name of Madame Alexandre, ran with her magisterial hand a famous hostelry, to which the princes of the Far East came in order to bring her their gold.

Verminous and clad in impure rags, "no longer having a brass farthing in his pocket and nothing in the bank," he therefore descended upon her one day, when fortune favored him to the extent to which her highness the pasha-ess, although enraged by his advent, was obliged to welcome him with the most ostentatious demonstrations of love.

The latter's bad luck determined, in fact, that at the very moment when, in defiance of all her instructions, he threw himself into her arms, she happened to be in conference with rigid senators incapable of making mock of the fourth commandment of divine law. One of them, moved to his entrails by that poignant incident, even thought he ought not to dispense with giving her his blessing and a prediction of eternal life.

After such a coup, Papa Ferdinand became impossible to dislodge, and permanently inextirpable. Under pain of incurring the indignation of honest folk and losing the fruitful esteem of the mandarins, it was necessary to clean him up, dress him, lodge him and fill him up every day.

Madame Alexandre's existence, previously as sweet as honey, was poisoned. That father was the thorn in her side, the fly in her ointment, the finger in her eye, and, unlike Calypso, she did not succeed in consoling herself with regard to Ulysses' return.

He was no trouble, though. From the very first day, he had been installed in the most remote, most uncomfortable and probably unhealthiest attic of number 12. He was hardly ever seen. He faithfully obeyed the instruction not to wander around the house at the times when clients called, and especially never to set foot in the reception-room.

It was necessary nonetheless to depart from that severe law when the whim of a foreign amateur sometimes asked to see the Old Man, about whom all the ladies spoke in murmurs of fearful veneration, as they might have talked about the Man in the Iron Mask.

For those occasions, he had a scarlet braided jerkin and a kind of Macedonian cap, which made him look like a Hungarian or Pole fallen on hard times. He was then ornamented with the title of Comte—Comte Boutonski!—and passed for a relic of the most recent insurrection, covered in glory.

Cumulatively, he cleaned the toilets, swept the staircases, and wiped the pans and the crockery—sometimes with the same dish-cloth, said Madame Alexandre, furiously. Finally, he ran errands for the boarders, whose confidence he enjoyed, and who gave him good tips.

In his leisure hours, the fortunate old man retired to his room and assiduously reread the works of Paul de Kock or the humanitarian lucubrations of Eugène Transpire,[1] as he called the author of *Les Mystères de Paris* and *Le Juif Errant*, the two best books in the world.

---

1 Eugène Sue. *Suer* means "to sweat," while *transpirer* means "to perspire," and in polite society, as everyone knows, only horses sweat, while men perspire and women merely glow.

During the war, naturally, the house was in a bad way. The clients were in the provinces or on the ramparts, and the state of siege rendered the sidewalks impracticable. Madame Alexandre's exasperation was at its peak. From morning until night she never ceased to exhale her fury against the Old Man, which became increasingly harsh and which she vomited forcefully and incessantly.

She went so far in her delirium as to accuse him of having ignited the international conflict with his machinations. When the ransom of five billions was determined, she claimed that she was being defrauded, protesting that her business was done for and that all old swine who brought bad luck should be put up against a wall and shot. . . .

She became positively rabid, and life became impossible.

It goes without saying that the Commune did not help to reinvigorate her tottering trade. The clientele did not go on strike—the establishment was never empty; one might have thought it was a church—but what a clientele! God in Heaven! Red-faced drunks, murderers, infamous hooligans braided from top to toe, who demanded service with revolver in hand and broke everything, and would have burned everything if anyone had had the audacity to resist them.

Then, of course, the bawd shut her mouth; she perished silently of fright, awaiting rescue from On High.

She did not have long to wait. The news suddenly spread that Versailles was about to enter Paris. Deliverance! But the poor creature was dogged by truly terrible luck. A barricade was set up at the end of the street. It was a time, if ever there was one, to triple-lock the door and play dead. Papa Ferdinand was completely forgotten.

The barricade was stormed at two o'clock in the afternoon and the fleeing federates abandoned the quarter. Soon, only one single person remained: a thin old man whose footsteps echoed in the great silence.

It was impossible not to recognize him. It was the dotard, who had gone out that morning out of curiosity and was stupidly fleeing like a criminal before the red-trousered troops.

The latter, full of suspicion, were not yet following him, hesitant to fire on a man of such great age. They came running, though, on seeing him stop at the door of number 12.

"Stand still and put your hands up."

The old man, panting with terror, hurled himself at the bell and started ringing it madly.

"Titine! Titine! It's me. Let your old father in!"

A shuttered window in the house of ill-repute opened then, spontaneously, and Madame Alexandre, drunk with joy, pointed at her father, shouting to the soldiers: "Shoot him, damn it! He was with the others just now. He's a dirty communard, an arsonist who tried to set fire to the quarter."

No more was required in those courteous days, and Papa Ferdinand, riddled with bullets, collapsed on the threshold. . . .

Today, Madame Alexandre has retired from business and is no longer resident in the neighborhood of the Bourse, of which she was for such a long time the glory. She has an annual income of thirty thousand francs, weighs four hundred kilos and reads the novels of Paul Bourget with great emotion.

Monsieur Pleur's Religion

Generally, the individuals who have excited
my disgust in this world were flourishing men
of good reputation. As for the rogues I have known,
who are not small in number, I think of all of them,
without exception, with pleasure and benevolence.

Thomas De Quincey

To Paul Adam[1]

THE appearance of the old man was suggestive of fecund vermin. The dung-heap of his soul was so obvious on his hands and face that it would not have been possible to imagine a more frightful contact. When he went through the streets, the filthiest gutter-streams, trembling as they reflected his image, appeared to want to reverse their flow.

His fortune, which was said to be so colossal that reliable judges could not estimate it without weeping with

---

1 Paul Adam (1862) was a prolific novelist who switched his primary allegiance from Naturalism to Symbolism in the 1890s but is nowadays best known for his historical novels set in the Napoleonic era. "La Religion de M. Pleur" was originally published in the 5 août 1893 issue of *Gil Blas*.

ecstasy, must have been hidden in extremely strange places, for no one dared hazard a firm guess about the nightmare's financial investments. It was only rumored that, on several occasions, his cadaverous hand was glimpsed in certain shady monetary dealings that had ended in sublime debacles, of which a few crooked bankers supposed him to be the artisan.

He was not a Jew, however, and when anyone suggested that he was a blackguard he had a mild manner of replying "God help you!" that made a slight shiver run down the spine of the most cunning.

The one thing that seemed certain was that the frightful bundle of rags owned a high-rent house in one of the great eccentric quarters. No one knew exactly where. Perhaps he owned several of them.

Legend said that he bedded down in some obscure lair, under the service stairway, between the latrine-pipe and the concierge's lodge, reducing the latter to idiocy by his proximity.

The receipts he issued for rent-payments were, I've been told, thriftily scribbled on torn-up posters, which tenants replete with the social graces sold on to astute collectors.

The tale was also told, and became famous, of a fantastic soup brewed regularly every Sunday evening, and which had to nourish him all week. In order not to waste coal, he ate it cold for six days in succession. By Tuesday, naturally, that alimentary substance became fetid. Then, with the reverent manner of a priest opening a tabernacle, he took from a little cupboard set in the wall, which must have contained strange papers, a bottle of exceedingly old rum, probably collected from some shipwreck. He poured a few

17

tiny drops into a minuscule glass and fortified himself in the expectation of savoring them immediately after having swallowed his cataplasm.

When the operation was complete, he said: "Now you've eaten your soup, you can't have your little glass of rum!" And dishonestly, he poured the precious liquid back into the bottle—a commendable delicacy that had always succeeded, for thirty or forty years.

Never had a specter seemed so completely devoid of style and character. Although he resembled, by virtue of his rags, and doubtless some of his practices, the most despised Jews of Budapest or Amsterdam, the imagination of a Prometheus could not have discovered the slightest archaic feature in him. The nickname of Shylock, awarded to him by subaltern insult-mongers, seemed a blasphemy, so platitudinous was its expression in his regard. There was nothing terrible about him but dirtiness and his stink, like a sick animal—but that too was a disheartening modernism. His filth would not have made him welcome in any abyss.

He merely realized, in appearance, the mediocre bourgeois—the "swan-killer," as Villiers put it,[1] accomplished and definitively evolved, such as he will appear at the end of days, when Earthquakes will bring vile souls out of their lairs to be manifest in broad daylight.

If one could claim innocence of the prostitution of words, it would have been necessary to compare Monsieur Pleur to the annunciator of God's vomit. He seemed to

---

1 "Le Tueur de cygnes" (1887; tr. as "The Swan-Killer") is one of several short stories by Villiers featuring the eponymous anti-hero of *Tribulat Bonhomet* (collection 1908); the character is a scathing parody of the supposed pretentions and narrow-mindedness of the contemporary bourgeois.

be saying to comfortable individuals disgusted by his presence: "Don't you understand, my brothers, that I am translating you for eternity, and that my impure carcass reflects you prodigiously? When the truth comes out, you will discover, once and for all, that I was your true fatherland, to such an extent that, once I'm gone, the pestilence of your minds will miss me. You'll be nostalgic about my filthy proximity, which made you seem to be alive, although you were below the level of the dead. Dirty hypocrites who detest in me the silent denunciation of your turpitudes, the material horror that I inspire in you is the precise measure of the abomination of your thoughts. For in the end, with what could I be verminous, if not with you, who are swarming in the depths of my heart?"

The eccentric's gaze was particularly unbearable to elegant women, whom he appeared to execrate, sometimes fixing them with a stare paler than the phosphors of charnel-houses: a funeral and viscous glance that stuck to their flesh like the saliva of a vampire, and drove them away yelping in fright.

"Isn't it true, darling," they thought they could hear, "that you're coming to meet me? I'll have you visit my gracious ditch and you'll see the pretty jewelry of snails and black beetles that I'll give you to heighten the whiteness of your divine skin. I'm as smitten with you as a venereal ulcer, and my kisses, I assure you, are better than any divorce. For you'll rot one day, my pink mouse; you'll rot voluptuously beside me, and we'll be two incense-burners under the stars. . . ."

But it would have been difficult, once again, in spite of that atrocious gaze, to indentify any feature that might have been said to be characteristic of Monsieur Pleur. The voice alone, perhaps: a voice of menacing softness, which suggested the idea of an indecent sacristan whispering ignominies.

For example, he had a way of pronouncing the word *"argent"* that abolished the notion of that metal, and even its representative value. One heard something like *erge* or *orge*, according to circumstance.[1] Often, in fact, one heard nothing at all: the word vanished. It was like a kind of sudden modesty, a curtain suddenly falling in front of sanctuary, an untimely dread of seeming obscene or despoiling the idol.

Imagine, if it amuses you, a fanatical sculptor, a sanguinary and mealy-mouthed Pygmalion, seeking with you the best viewpoint from which to see his Galatea, and slyly causing you to move backwards toward an open trap-door ready to swallow you up.

It was so strong, that jealous passion for *Argent*, that some people were deceived by it. Horrible vices were attributed to that impenitent devotee of the money-box and the safe—unjust suspicions, but accredited by a few savant exegetists of the private lives of others, who had glimpsed him in mysterious conversation with women or children on the sidewalk.

His worship was sometimes expressed in such ecstatic circumlocutions, the drooling erethism of his fervor attenuated his withered gravedigger's physiognomy so strangely, and such dishonest sighs were then exhaled from his bosom, that the vessels of last resort into which he let his

---

1 I have left the key word in this passage untranslated because the double meaning of the French *argent*—silver and money—cannot be fully reproduced in English, and substituting "money" would obliterate the oblique wordplay of the abbreviation *orge* [barley].

rare words fall could, after all, be excused for merely sensing the passage between him and them of the hypochondriac majesty of Idolatry.

I may be excused, I hope, from explaining the exceptional reasons that determined a commerce of amity between myself and this sympathetic individual. I was young then—very young, even—and easily accessible to enthusiasm. Monsieur Pleur took pleasure in saturating me with it by unveiling himself to me.

I thought I was alone in receiving his confidences. I will add that the memory in question has been a great help to me in supporting a destiny worse than beastly, and, the man in question having now been dead for a long time, my conscience now urges me to testify in favor of that misunderstood individual.

A few men of my generation can recall his tragic end, which arrived in the last days of the Empire, and which caused quite a stir.

The murder, of which the newspapers brought me details as far away as Cap Nord, was certainly of the most banal sort, and its villainous perpetrators were, it must be admitted, unworthy of the celebrity they obtained. The old man had simply been strangled in his rat-hole by bandits previously devoid of notoriety, who had no other motive than theft—but certain circumstances solely related to the victim's past, which remained inexplicable, exercised the sagacity of his contemporaries in vain for some months.

Finally, they thought that they had divined or understood that Monsieur Pleur was not what he appeared to be.

In brief, the luckless murderers—who had, moreover, allowed themselves to be caught with extreme facility—had not been able to discover the slightest treasure in the

miser's lair, and, although the latter died intestate and without natural heirs, the State could not gets its claws on any
property, movable or unmovable.

It was established that the defunct possessed absolutely
nothing—except for a annuity deriving from a life-interest
in a gigantic fortune unassailably alienated in the hands of
a certain bishop.

It was impossible to discover what had become of
the considerable sums that must have passed through his
hands during the many years that he handed out receipts
to the squadrons of tenants: there was not a single bond
or share certificate; only the famous bottle of rum, emp-
tied by the stranglers,

As this is hardly a tale, I have the right not to promise
a more dramatic conclusion; I repeat that I only want to
offer my testimony, probably the only one for which the
angry shade of the dead man can hope.

Allow me, then, to summarize in a few lines the rather
curious words that were spoken to me, several times, by
that ordinarily silent recluse. I do not think I ever felt such
a sinister frisson as on that distant day when, as we sat side
by side on a bench in the Jardin des Plantes, he told me
this:

"My avarice scares you. Well, my lad, I once knew a
prodigal, of a species less rare than one might think, whose
story might give you a desire to kiss my rags respectfully, if
you have enough intelligence to understand it.

"This prodigal was a maniac—naturally. That's always
easy to say, and dispenses with any profound analysis. He
was even, if you like, a monomaniac. His obsession was to
throw bread into latrines.

"He ruined several bakers to that end. One never met him without a large stick of bread under his arm, hurrying along, with a spring in his step, amid the banter of the populace.

"He only lived to accomplish that action, and it's necessary to believe that he obtained furious enjoyments from it—but his joy became a delirium when the opportunity presented itself to offer the spectacle to poor devils dying of starvation.

"He had an annual income of thirty thousand francs, that fellow, and complained about the high price of bread.

"Meditate on that story attentively, which resembles an apologue."

I had no desire to kiss Monsieur Pleur's rags, but his story was doubtless sufficiently clear to me, for I thought I heard the entire cavalry of the abyss galloping beneath me.

The last time I encountered that Plato of stinginess, he said to me: "Do you know that *Argent* is God, and that it's for that reason that people seek it so ardently? You don't, do you?—you're too young to have thought of it. You'd undoubtedly take me for some kind of sacrilegious madman if I told you that He is infinitely good, infinitely perfect, the sovereign Lord of all things, and that nothing can be done in this world without His order and His permission—and that, in consequence, we have been created uniquely to know Him, adore Him and serve Him, and by that means to earn Eternal Life. You'd be nauseated if I talked to you about the mystery of His Incarnation. No matter! Know that I never let a day go by without wondering when His Reign will come and His Name will be sanctified.

"I also ask *Argent*, my Redeemer, to deliver me from all evil, all sin, the Devil's snares, the spirit of fornication, and I implore Him by virtue of His idleness as well by virtue of His Joys and His Glory.

"You will understand one day, my boy, how that God has debased Himself for us. Remember my maniac! And see to what employment the Malice of men condemns Him!

"Personally, I haven't dared touch Him for thirty years. Yes, young man, for thirty years I haven't dared to put my dirty hands on a fifty-centime piece! When my tenants pay me, I receive their money in a precious olive-wood box, which has touched the Tomb of Christ, and I don't keep it for a single day.

"I am, if you want to know, a penitent of Argent. With inexpressible consolations, I endure for Him being despised by people, even frightening animals, and being crucified every day of my life by the most frightful poverty. . . ."

I had sufficiently penetrated the mysterious existence of that extraordinary man to grasp that he was talking to me in an entirely symbolic fashion. Even so, I confess that sacred language, so rudely adapted, scared me a little.

He stood up suddenly, raised his arms, and I can still see him standing there, like a double gibbet from which the rotten remains of some ancient victim of execution were hanging.

"It's said often enough," he cried, "that I'm a horrible miser. Well, you'll be able to tell them, one day, that I've discovered a hiding place, infinitely secure, that no other miser before me has yet perceived.

"I bury my money in the Bosom of the Poor!

"Publish that, my child, on the day when Scorn and Dolor have given you the supreme honor of being misunderstood."

Monsieur Pleur nourished some two hundred families, among whom you would search in vain for an individual who did not regard him as a rogue, so cunning was he.

But today, just Heaven, what has become of the pale multitude of indigents assisted by the Episcopal delegation of that Penitent?

The Tarantulas' Parlor

To P. N. Roinard[1]

IT was at Barbey d'Aurevilly's home in 1869, in the days of my radiant youth, that I met the poet. He interested me immediately by virtue of his hair and his loud mouth.

He had a white hirsuteness that made his head seem like an ongoing challenge to all barbers. Although he was barely forty, his thick snowy fleece that quivered in the wind gave him the appearance, at a distance, of a petulant Saturn or a thunderous Jupiter prematurely aged by an incredible abuse of the windows of voluptuousness.

The wretched little face of crushed brick that he exhibited beneath that blizzard was boiled and baked to a greater degree every time one looked at it. His chromic agitation even astonished him. "I'm in the tarantulas' parlor!" he would cry, in his voice, ripe for a straight-jacket—

---

1 Paul-Napoléon Roinard (1856-1930) was a poet, dramatist and painter, nowadays remembered for his experimental attempt to introduced perfumes as a supplement to theatrical performance and his exhibition of paintings of "the great men of the future," which depicted literary men as they might look when aged; it got a poor reception and he shelved plans for complementary exhibitions of musicians and scientists. He was a co-founder with Zo d'Axa of the original version of the Anarchist periodical *L'En-dehors* (1891-93). "Le Parloir des tarentules" was originally published in the 12 août 1893 issue of *Gil Blas*.

which made little seamstresses increase their pace in the street. He always had the air of a Samson bursting ropes or shackles with which naïve Philistines had tried to bind him while he slept.

The unfortunate d'Aurevilly, who was one day to succumb in the web of a black spider of Languedocian occultism, had no hesitation in igniting the rage of that volcanic metromane, who was decidedly incapable of accepting a consideration, even distinguished, that was not the first, or better still, the only one. [1]

Damascène Chabrol had been a physician—or rather, still was, for it is said that medicine imprints a character as surely as the priesthood. Having no absolute need to earn a living, however, he had soon lost his taste for purging businessmen or analyzing their secretions. In consequence, he had vomited up his clientele—not to employ a stronger term of which he made frequent usage—and had generously devoted himself to the most intensive cultivation of verse.

I believed, at the time, that he was not entire unworthy of taking up the lyre, and if my memory is accurate, that was the opinion of a few authorities. God knows what I would think of him today! But life is so short, alas, and of such uncertain duration, that I would truly dread to wear through the precious fabric of my existence by seeking out, beneath the accumulated dust of twenty-five years, the two or three forgotten collections that he published.

---

1 The reference to "a black spider of Languedocian occultism" probably refers to the Lyon-born would-be Rosicrucian magus Joséphin Péladan, whose salon Barbey attended and who became one of Bloy's bitterest enemies. A metromane is a person whose mania is writing verses.

I will add that, even supposing that he had genius, no poem written by his hand could ever have equaled the unmatchable poem of the night we spent together at his home in the Rue de Fleurus four days before his terrible death, and which was not—I beg you to be unshakably convinced—a night of love.

Three wild passions lived within him: pretty women, great verses and the desire for glory. Each of them having the undeniable characteristics of paroxysm, I have never really understood how they could persist together— especially the first with the other two.

It was a funereal thing, the enthusiasm of that man, like a possessed patriarch, for the sluts and chits adored by the late Sainte-Beuve, who at least had nothing patriarchal about him, and it was a benefit of the Second Empire that the violence of his sudden fantasies had always been able to be deadened in the neighboring cheap lodging-houses or the thickets of the Luxembourg without any troublesome scandal.

In the intervals between these crises, while waiting for the goat to resurface within him, he threw himself into writing, hurling himself into the whirlwinds of inspiration like a petrel in a storm—and then there was a host of visions, of semi-visions, of hot lightning-flashes, of total eclipses, of blasphemies gesticulated against the irresponsible vault of heaven, and invocations whispered familiarly into the ears of all demons, until the moment when he sprawled on his carpet, grinding his teeth, writhing in epileptic convulsions.

It was difficult to be introduced into his home. He always seemed to be afraid that something subtle, infinitely rare and precious might escape through the open door, descend the staircase, slip past the morose concierge and go profane itself amid the infinite shame of the dogs in the streets.

In consequence, he did not open the door when anyone knocked, or, if he did open it, it was only by a crack, holding the door a millimeter from the door-post and, with is free hand, sketching broad gestures demanding silence, as if there were a sublime invalid dying in there, for whom the perfect equilibrium of the universe was necessary in order not to disturb their last sigh.

And if the visitor, not frightened off by the fiery eyes of the recluse, wanted to pass anyway, in spite of that strange welcome, he could never introduce himself too rapidly, and the door would close abruptly at that very instant, like a rat-trap on a shrew. That was a rare temerity of which few men, I assure you, were capable.

Then the redoubtable Damascène, bent over, rubbed his hands, fingertips downwards and the palms close to his chin, expressing thus the delight of a cannibal over his prey—and the fanfare of his recriminations would burst forth for an hour. It became a torrent of complaint, of which one heard, first of all, the dull rumble and swelling rumor as it arrived, in the distance from the blue mountains; then the raucous roar of increasing clarity, which spread out like an immense sheet; and finally the enormous din of the dislocations and collapses it occasioned, of all their clamors confused.

The flow was truly wholehearted—and I suppose that it would have required the intervention of death for him to cease to vociferate, until he went to sleep, against editors, newspapers, the Academy, the associates of the Comédie-Française, and, in general, against the entire human clique that was stubborn in its refusal to reward him.

Perhaps he was right. I repeat that I don't know, and that I don't want to know. I'm sufficiently intoxicated by my own indignation, without needing to get drunk on that of others.

I'll get to the poem of that night, the most famous of all, which was not a night of love.

Very exceptionally, Damascène Chabrol had invited me by letter to come to see him, not for dinner, which would have been merely salutary, and, in consequence, utterly banal, but to hear him read one of his dramas—which appeared to me to be dangerous and very frightening.

His letter, moreover, much more comminatory than fraternal, left me in no possible doubt about the gravity of the matter. He absolutely demanded that I be punctual, declaring that justice required it.

That form of invitation did not revolt me. My curiosity, keenly excited, immediately established an accord between justice and my will. I was punctual—and this, quite simply, is what happened.

At the first knock, the door opened slightly, and I was introduced, in accordance with the abovementioned ritual.

Damascène was calmer than I had dared to hope. He was even prodigiously calm, and I could not help comparing him to a surgeon or an executioner about to fulfill his function—an analogy whose rigor I was infinitely far from suspecting.

Two toddies had been prepared, and on the table, wide open in front of one of the two chairs, the redoubtable manuscript was displayed.

The weather was mild, fortunately. If it had been too cold or too hot, I might very well have died that night, the most obvious precautions having been taken in order that I should understand the absolute futility of any attempted interruption, however brief or justified it might be.

"*La Fille de Jephté*, a Biblical drama in five acts,"[1] he began, fixing me with an implacable stare.

The exercise, at first, did not displease me. The reader had a bizarre gastralgic voice, rising effortlessly from *basso profundo* to the most childishly high-pitched notes. He spoke thus, and veritably acted out his drama, multiplying his gestures to the point of throwing himself to his knees for a prayer when the situation demanded it: a curious spectacle that amused me for an hour—which is to say, throughout the first act, alone, for the monster took conscientiousness so far as to recommence entire scenes, of which he was afraid that he had not communicated the full beauty to me, several times over, without any admiring protest being able to reassure him.

In the second act, the performance having lost the charm of the unexpected, I actually began to listen properly.

It was lamentable. Imagine the dustiest, most worn-out, soiled and most fetid hackwork—a rightful amalgam of Racine, the amiable Gagne and Désaugiers.[2] I remember an interminable speech by its impossible Judge about agriculture and social economy. . . .

Toward the end of the third act, I feigned a sudden need of the most vulgar sort, hoping thus to reach the door to the stairway. The damnable man accompanied me. . . .

---

1 Based on the story told in *Judges* 11: 31-40; the character is known as Jephthah in English versions of the Old Testament.
2 Paulin Gagne (1808-1876) and Marc-Antoine Desaugiers (1772-1827)

It was necessary to swallow the whole thing, and it lasted until midnight. I was almost as sacrificed as the daughter of the Liberator of Israel herself. But imagine how I felt, as I launched myself toward my hat, when Damascène, in words that seemed to me to be drawn from the Apocalypse, said: "Oh, don't hurry—we haven't read anything yet. I'm not letting you go before you've heard my sonnets."

Someone ignorant of the French language might have thought that he was offering me a cup of chocolate. He set out to recite *fifteen hundred* sonnets—more than twenty thousand lines—and his voice, far from being enfeebled by his preceding effort, was now even clearer, fresher, better pitched: capable it seemed of trumpeting until the fall, so unfortunately postponed, of the heavens.

What could I do? It was clear to me that I could only get out over the dead body of that madman, and I did not then have the venial habit of dipping my hands in blood that I acquired subsequently.

I pulled myself together, stifling a groan of despair.

Five minutes later, I was profoundly asleep. The carillon of an Alpine cow-bell, fervently agitated close to my ear, woke me up again.

"Aha! I believe you were asleep," said my executioner.

"My God," I replied. "I dozed off without going to sleep. I confess that I feel a little tired."

"All right—I understand."

He opened his drawer then and took out a revolver, which appeared to me to be abnormal in its dimensions, carefully loaded it, rested it on the table without letting go of the butt, picked up his manuscript in his left hand, and simply said: "I'll go on."

That torture lasted until sunrise. Then he got up mechanically, closed his file of papers and declared that he was going to catch a train.

"I'm going to see Papa," he said.

A few hours later, on arriving in Orléans, he slapped his sixty-year-old father across the face and immediately went to throw himself down a well, from the bottom of which he was hauled up, raving mad, and locked in a padded cell, where he died in mid-frenzy two days later.

To my extreme surprise, I inherited a considerable fraction of his fortune, and it is, if anyone cares, with his money that I amused myself so much between the ages of twenty-five and thirty, as everyone knows.

Plan For a Funeral Oration

To Gustave de Malherbe[1]

ONLY a few people know that he has died. When the multitude of those who think that he is still alive learn of his death there will surely be vivid clichéd jeremiads in the newspapers about the great writer "whom it is painful to have lost," after having been so basely detested during his life.

Those univocal and professional lamentations will be heaped on with a shovel, like cemetery soil, by the gravediggers of the news, all the way to the feet of the "friend who was with him at the end," a briny and vulpine romancer who had need of that renown and who confiscated his final agony, making his death even more bitter.

Let us be content simply to name him Lazarus, that person who died in the most perfect ignorance, but who had the right to bear one of the largest comtal crowns in the Occident.

---

1 The publisher Gustave de Malherbe (1856-1934) was one of Bloy's friends and correspondents, but does not appear to have published any of his works. "Projet d'oraison funèbre" was originally published in the 25 août 1893 issue of *Gil Blas*. "Lazarus" is a transfiguration of Villiers de l'Isle Adam.

"I am," he said, "of the race of Beings who do honor to other men."

He never wanted anyone to talk to him about "any other fatherland than exile," and life, in consequence, was extremely hard for that poor sublime devil.

In due course, when the sham flames of that blaze of posthumous admiration have gone out—sooner or later—I shall talk about that dead man, whose sadness and horror, carefully hidden, would be difficult to surpass; for I can assure you that I have a lot to say, and the black matter is superabundant.

That is not exactly my objective today. I only wish, with respect to this Lazarus, whom everyone has the right to suppose imaginary, to verify with the light of a deplorable torch the most decisive adage regarding the old aristocracies that the Revolution was supposed to have killed off: "Every man is the sum of his breeding."

Thus was the experience of centuries condensed, like a bronze blade, by the philosopher Blanc de Saint Bonnet.[1] It means that, at the extremity of the most recent branch of a great tree selected by the lightning, there always hangs a fruit of delectation or terror, in which the precious essence makes a port of call before disappearing forever.

When it is a matter of a glorious sap, as in the case of our Lazarus, the dolorous individual charged with assuming full responsibility is not only the unique support of the splendors or miseries, divine joys or profound griefs, abasements or triumphs accumulated by so many ancestors. He must also bear the Dream of all that, which he bears into the long, interminable desert, "the uterus of

---

1 Antoine Blanc de Saint Bonnet (1815-1880) was an ultramontane philosopher who had a considerable influence on Barbey d'Aurevilly.

the sepulcher," without a single soul being able to help or console him.

It is necessary for him to submit to the miraculous and redoubtable heritage of a breast swollen with all the sighs of generation, whose very name is in its death-throes—and, my God, that is not all, for this is the abyss of dolors.

The destiny of Lazarus was so extraordinary that his life appeared to be a condensation of the history of the noble family whose supreme incarnation he was. A kind of analogy will perhaps make that comprehensible.

Do you recall those exemplary chronologies that pedagogues unsated with maledictions inflicted upon us in our childhood? Every epoch is condemned to respire between four narrow pages these suffocating opuscules in which the most distant and the most distinct events are piled up and pressed like salted herrings in an exporter's barrel.

Charlemagne is mingled there with the Merovingians, the first Valois are merely a filling, along with the Valois d'Orléans and the Valois d'Angoulême, Henri III is digging into the ribs of Charles le Sage, François I is flattened against Louis le Gros, Ravillac is assassinating Jean Sans Peur and it's at Varennes that Louis XIV seems to be signing the revocation of the Edict of Nantes. Etc. Any perspective is impossible and the chaos inextricable.

Lazarus, the last of his name, no longer having anything before him but the increasing boorishness of the *fin-de-siècle*, was himself, in a way, one of those terrible digests.

Incapable of adjusting to contemporary life, which filled him with disgust, he resided in the depths of his own heart, like some antediluvian dragon in his lair, haggard and inconsolable regarding the destruction of his species.

He really did bear within him the souls of all the great men of his House, and the list was a long one. He confabulated with their shades, not seeking disrespectfully to disentangle them—quite the opposite—and ending up no longer knowing what went back, in all justice, to each of them.

He was, in any case, one of those rare adepts who deny death, persuading himself that survival is a simple act of will, and that it is incomparably easier to eternalize oneself than to come to an end.

In his view, the death of which so many imbeciles speak is nothing but an imposture, an untenable imposture invented by the manufacturers of crowns and tombstones. He had even written, for his own personal amusement, a fantasy—Hegelian, alas!—on that subject, with a view to establishing that beings and things can have no other preservation in the face of Infinity than that which it pleases our consciousness to accord to them.

He lived, therefore, in the midst of a superb group, whose resurrection he had obtained a long time ago, unworried about bringing together warriors and magistrates separated by the breadth of centuries, whose very personalities were lost for him in he admirable host of individuals of his blood.

The infernal existence of the man is sufficiently well-known. A marvelous legend has been compiled in his regard, although bizarre circumstances, with which the imagination of a few has maliciously overloaded him, were much rarer, in reality, than people suppose.

The celebrated disturbance of his mind was nothing, fundamentally, but the disturbance of his poor soul, and as such, was tragic enough.

I have said that his life was configured by the history of his family, and that that gave rise to an unspeakable dolor, but how does such a language make itself heard? The history that is at the core of universal history, which one learns so poorly in schools, was, in him, entirely alive and contemporary; it burned him, devoured him like a furious flame whose final fuel he was.

In the conflagration of tortures, his slightest actions immediately recuperated the ancient deeds of the entire quasi-royal lineage that was dying on its feet in the ventricles of his heart.

Very few people understood him, and what could they do for such a grandiose unfortunate? God himself, the God Moloch, no longer wanting aristocracy, the holocaust was unavoidable.

Literary genius had been given to him as a bonus, but that was the trifle of his torture.

How beautiful his beginnings had been! One was twenty years old, one dazzled men and women, all fanfares burst forth on all thresholds; one brought something new into the world, something totally unprecedented, which the world would doubtless adore, since it was the reflection, the faithful intaglio, of primitive Idols. What did it matter that one was very poor? Was that not one grandeur more? One had, in any case, a bag full of fruits that resembled stars, picked by the handful in the luminous forest, and one did not doubt the human species.

But one perceived, one day, that the people, tired of bread, were shouting for apples, that they wanted the soles of their feet to be rubbed with the grease of the small intestines of the Princes of Light—and that was the commencement of an agony that lasted thirty years

It had too many witnesses for its description to be necessary. In any case, my courage is wanting. I shall keep to myself, as I said above, the last and unknown final phase—the one, very profoundly unknown, I assure you, of which I want to be the implacable publisher. We shall then see the color of the face of a certain pontiff.

The Captives of Longjumeau

To Madame Henriette L'Huillier[1]

THE *Postillon de Longjumeau* announced the deplorable deaths of the two Fourmis yesterday. That paper, justly reputed for the abundance and quality of its information, lost itself in conjectures regarding the mysterious causes of the despair that had driven those two spouses, who were believed to be happy, to suicide.

Married very young, and still in their honeymoon twenty years later, they had not left the town for a single day.

Freed by the foresight of their authors from all the financial anxieties that can poison conjugal life, they were, on the contrary, amply provided with what was necessary to add pleasure to a union that, although undoubtedly legitimate, was little in conformity with the need for amorous vicissitudes that ordinarily harass versatile humans. They personified, in the eyes of the world, the miracle of perpetual affection.

One evening in May, the day after the fall of Monsieur Thiers, the suburban train had brought them, with their

1 Henriette L'Huillier was one of Bloy's correspondents for many years; samples of their correspondence were published in 2012. "Les Captives de Longjumeau" was originally published in the 1 septembre 1893 issue of *Gil Blas*.

parents, to take up residence in the delightful property that was to shelter their joy. The pure-hearted Longjumellians had watched the lovely couple—whom the veterinarian did not hesitate to compare to Paul and Virginie—pass by with affection. They were, in fact, genuinely looking well that day, resembling two pale children of the nobility.

Maître Piécu, the most important notary in the canton, had acquired for them, when they came to the town, a nest of verdure that the dead would have envied them—for it is necessary to admit that the garden was reminiscent of an abandoned cemetery. That appearance did not displease them, undoubtedly, since they did not make any immediate changes, and let the vegetation grow freely.

To make use of a profoundly original expression of Maître Piécu's, they lived "in the clouds," seeing hardly anyone, not out of malice or disdain but simply because they never thought about it. Then, it would be necessary to disentangle themselves for a few hours or a few minutes, to interrupt their ecstasy—and believe me, in view of the brevity of life, those extraordinary spouses did not have the courage to do that.

One of the great men of the Middle Ages, Maître Jean Tauler,[1] tells the story of a recluse to whom a importunate visitor came in order to ask for some object that was in his cell. The recluse dutifully went inside to fetch the object, but once inside he forgot what it was, because the image of exterior things could not remain in is mind. He therefore went out and asked the visitor what he wanted. The latter repeated his request. The recluse went back in, but before picking up the object, he had lost his memory

---

1 The mystic theologian Jean Tauler (c130-1361) was a Dominican renowned for his studies of neo-Platonism.

of it. After several attempts he was obliged to say to the importunate: "Go in and look for what you need yourself, for I cannot keep your image in mind long enough to do what you ask."

Monsieur and Madame Fourmi often reminded me of that recluse. They would have gladly given anyone anything that was asked of them, if they had been able to remember it for a single instant.

Their distraction was famous; it was talked about all the way to Corbeil. However, they did not seem to be suffering, and the "deadly" resolution that had terminated their generally-envied existence seemed inexplicable.

An already-old letter from the unfortunate Fourmi, whom I had known before his marriage, permitted me to reconstitute, by means of induction, the whole lamentable story. This, then, is the letter in question. Perhaps you will see that my friend was neither a madman or an imbecile.

> *For the tenth or twentieth time, my dear friend, we have failed to keep our word outrageously. However patient you might be, I imagine that you must be weary of inviting us. The truth is that this time, as with the preceding ones, my wife and I have no excuses. We had written telling you to expect us, and we had absolutely nothing to do. However, we missed the train, as usual.*
>
> *For five years now we have missed every train and every public carriage, no matter what we do. It's infinitely idiotic, and atrociously ridiculous, but I'm beginning to believe that the malady is incurable. It's a kind of ludicrous fatality, of which we are the victims. Nothing can to be done about it. Sometimes, for instance, we've got up at three o'clock in the morning,*

or even stayed up all night, in order not to miss the eight o'clock train. Well, my dear chap, the chimney caught fire at he last moment, I sprained an ankle half way, Juliette's dress caught on some bush, we went to sleep on the bench in the waiting-room without either the arrival of the train or the shouts of the employee waking us in time, etc., etc. The last time, I forgot my wallet. . . .

Finally, I repeat, this has been going on for fifteen years, and I sense that it will be the death of us. Because of it, as you know, I've made a mess of everything, I've quarreled with everyone, I'm regarded as a monster of selfishness, and my poor Juliette is naturally enveloped with the same reprobation. Since our arrival in this accursed place, I've missed seventy-four funerals, twelve marriages, thirty baptisms, and a thousand visits or indispensable meetings. I let my mother-in-law die without seeing her again a single time, although she was ill for nearly a year—and who deprived us of three-quarters of her succession, which she took away from us in rage by means of a codicil on the eve of her death.

I would never finish if I attempted to list the gaffes and misadventures occasioned by the incredible circumstance that we have never been able to get away from Longjumeau. To sum it all up in one word, we're captives, deprived henceforth of hope, and anticipating the moment when this galley-slave existence will become unbearable to us. . . .

I shall suppress the remainder, in which my sad friend confided things too intimate for me to be able to publish them—but I give you my word of honor that he was not a vulgar man, that he was worthy of the adoration of his wife, and that those two beings deserved better than to end their lives as stupidly and inappropriately as they did.

Certain details that I ask permission to keep to myself lead me to think that the unfortunate couple really were the victims of a tenebrous machination of the Enemy of humankind, who led them, by the hand of an evidently infernal notary, to that maleficent corner of Longjumeau, from which nothing had the power to extract them.

I truly believe that they were incapable of escaping therefrom, that there was an cordon of invisible troops around their dwelling, carefully selected to lay siege to them, and against whom no energy would have been capable of prevailing.

The sign for me of a diabolical influence is that the Fourmis were devoured by a passion for travel. Those captives were, by nature, essentially migratory. Before marrying, they had been avid to tour the world. While they were only engaged, they were seen at Enghien, at Choisy-le-Roi, at Meudon, at Clamart and at Montretout. One day they even went as far as Saint-Germain.

At Longjumeau, which appeared to them to be an Oceanic island, that rage for audacious exploration, adventures on land and sea, could only have been exasperated. Their house was cluttered with globes and planispheres; they had English and German atlases. They even possessed a map of the moon published in Gotha under the direction of a pedant named Justus Perthes.[1]

When they were not making love they read the stories of famous navigators together, with which their library

_____

1 The lunar map in question, published by Justus Perthes in 1880, was the work of Adolf Stieler.

was exclusively filled, and there was not a travel journal, a *Tour du Monde* or a Geographical Society Bulletin to which they were not subscribers. Railway timetables and the prospectuses of shipping companies rained down upon them unremittingly.

Believe it or not, their suitcases were always packed. They were always on the point of leaving, of undertaking an interminable voyage to the most distant, the most dangerous or the most unexplored lands. I received a good forty telegrams announcing their imminent departure for Borneo, Tierra de Fuego, New Zealand or Greenland.

Several times, in fact, they got within a hair's breadth of leaving—but in the end, they never left, because they could not and must not leave. Atoms and molecules collaborated to hold them back.

One day, however, ten years ago, they thought that they would definitely escape. They had succeeded, against all expectation, in hurling themselves into a first-class carriage that was to take them to Versailles. Deliverance! There, undoubtedly, the magic circle would be broken.

The train set off, but they did not budge. They were, of course, ensconced in a carriage designated to remain in the station. They had to begin all over again.

The only journey that they were unable to fail to make was evidently the one that they have just undertaken, alas, and the character that I know so well leads me to believe that they did not prepare for it without trembling.

A Bad Idea

To Louis Montchal,[1]
the dedicatee of *Le Désesperé*

THERE were four of them and I knew them very well. If that tells you absolutely nothing, we shall call them Théodore, Théodule, Théophile and Théophraste.

They were not brothers, but they lived together and never spent a minute apart. One could not see one of them without the other three immediately appearing.

The leader of the squadron, naturally, was Théophraste, the last-named, the man of *The Characters*,[2] and I think that he was worthy to command his companions, because he was able to command himself.

He was a strict puritan of sorts, harnessed to certainties, meticulous and attentive. Externally, he was simultaneously reminiscent of a badger and an assessor in a pawnbroker's shop in a poor district. When one said *bonjour* to

1 Louis Montchal (1853-1927) was another of Bloy's correspondents; some of the relevant letters are reprinted in he same 2012 volume as those relating to Henriette L'Huillier. "Une idée mediocre" was originally published in the 8 septembre 1893 issue of *Gil Blas*.
2 The Greek philosopher Theophrastus, who was active in the third century B.C. is credited (not entirely reliably) with authorship of *The Characters*, which consists of thirty outlines of social types.

him he always looked as if he were receiving a pledge, and his reply resembled an expert evaluation.

Internally, his soul was the stable of an inexorable mule, of the same species as those that are bred with so much care in England, or in the city of Calvin, for transporting whited coffins. He did not want people to think that he was a Protestant, however, and affirmed that he was Catholic to his fingertips, ostensibly hanging out his heart to dry on the poles of the Vine of the Elect.

His stock-in-trade was to be chaste, and, above all, to appear so: as chaste as a nail, as a pair of scissors, as a salted herring. His acolytes proclaimed him incorruptible and undefilable, no less white and lactescent than the radiant mantle of an angel.

Dare I say it? He regarded woman as disgusting, and telling him a lewd joke would have been the height of dementia. He disapproved in a general manner of the sexes coming together, and any reference to love seemed to him to be a personal attack.

He was so chaste that he would have forbidden zouaves to wear kilts.

Such, in broad terms, was the physiognomy of the leader. Allow me to sketch the others.

Théodore was the lion of the group. He was its pride and ornament, and it was him who came to the fore when it was a matter of diplomacy of persuasion, for Théophraste lacked eloquence. It is true that on those occasions, Théodore got drunk in order to roar better, but he acquitted himself to the general satisfaction.

He was a little Gascon lion, unfortunately devoid of a mane, who flattered himself on belonging to the celebrated family, almost extinct today of the Théodores of Saint-

Antonin and Lexos, of whom the banks of the Aveyron knew the glory.

It would have been impolite to be unaware of the fact that his coat-of-arms, the proud and noble coat-of-arms of his ancestors, was sculpted on the porch or some other place in the Cathedral of Albi or Carcassonne. The voyage was too expensive for anyone to undertake a verification, which was unnecessary, in any case, since he gave his word as a gentleman.

That coat-of-arms, carefully copied on tracing-paper at the Bibliothèque Nationale, were not shown to me, but the motto—*Par la sambleu!*—has always appeared to me to be as simple as it is magnificent.[1]

In brief, Théodore fascinated and dazzled his friends, whose ancestors were, alas, mere peasants. However, he could only be their corporal, because all brightness has to yield to wisdom. It was the dull but impeccable Théophraste who had united them into a sheaf in order that the storms of life could not break them. It was he who maintained them thus every day, educating them in virtue, teaching them to live and to think, and the hot-headed Achilles had nobly accepted obedience to the oracular Nestor.

Théodule and Théophile can be expedited in a few words. The first had nothing remarkable about him but the apparent robustness, of a docile and unconsciousness ox, who could easily have been made to labor in a cemetery. He was simply happy to march under the prod, and had had almost no need of light.

The second, by contrast, marched out of fear. He did not find the sheaf very lively or amusing, but having let

---

1 *Sambleu* is a weak oath, so the "motto" translates as something akin to "By Jove!" or "Damn it!"

himself be bound by Théophraste, he dared not even conceive the idea of a desertion, and trembled at the thought of displeasing that redoubtable man. He was a very young man, almost a child, who, I believe, merited a better fate, for he seemed to me to be endowed with intelligence and sensitivity.

Now, here is the wretched idea, the imbecilic wagon to which those four individuals were harnessed. If anyone can discover a worse one, I would be personally obliged if they would let me know what it is. They had decided to realize four-handed the mysterious association of the Thirteen dreamed up by Balzac[1]—a pagan dream if ever there was one. *Eadem velle, eadem nolle*, said Sallust, who was one of the most atrocious rogues of antiquity.[2]

To have but one soul and one brain divided within four epidermises—which is to say, in the final analysis, to renounce one's personality, to be become a number, a quantity, a package, fractions of a collective being. What a conception of genius! However, the wine of Balzac, too powerful for those poor heads, having intoxicated them, that state appeared to them to be divine, and they bound themselves together by oath.

You read that correctly—by oath! On what gospel, on what altar, on what relics? They did not tell me—unfortunately, because I would have been very curious to know that. All that I was able to discover or conjecture was that,

---

1 *Histoire des Treize* [The Story of the Thirteen] (1839) is a strange portmanteau novel by Balzac which combines three novellas linked by the theme of the secret society of the Treize, consisting of thirteen supernaturally like-minded individuals.
2 The actual quotation from Sallust's *Bellum Catalinae* is *Nam idem velle atque idem nolle, ea demum firma amticia est* [Liking the same things and disliking the same things is the only basis for a strong friendship].

by execratory formulas, the testimony of all the abysses being invoked, they vowed themselves to that absurd existence of never having a single thought that was not the thought of their group, of not loving or detesting anything that was not loved or detested in common, of never keeping the slightest secret, of reading all their letters and living together in perpetuity, without separating for a single day.

Naturally, Théophraste must have been the instigator of that solemn act. The others would not have gone so far.

All four being clerks in the same office of a ministry, it was possible for them to realize the essential part of the program. They would have the same lodgings, the same table, the same garments, the same creditors, the same strolls, the same reading materials, the same mistrust or horror of everything that was not their quadrille and would be mistaken in the same fashion about people and things.

In order to be entirely committed to one another they cut themselves off rudely from their former friends and benefactors, including a very great artist, whom they had had the incredible luck to interest momentarily, and who had tried to warn them against the tendency to walk on four feet like swine.

Years went by in that fashion—the best years of life, for the eldest, Théophraste, was scarcely thirty when the association commenced. They became almost famous. Ridicule dogged their steps to such an extent that they had to move to a new district several times.

Good people felt compassion on seeing those four sad men pass by, those slaves enchained by Stupidity, clad in the same manner and marching with the same step, who gave the impression of dragging their souls along the ground, watched attentively by suspicious policemen.

Naturally, it had to finish with a drama.

One day, the combustible Théodore fell in love.

They had as little communication with others as possible, but they did have some. A young woman whom God did not love thought that she would be doing well by marrying a gentleman whose coat of arms most certainly embellished the cathedral of Albi or the cathedral of Carcassonne.

I cannot, of course, recount the infinitely complicated story of that marriage, which modified in the most complete and profound manner the mechanical existence of our heroes.

At the first symptoms of the malady, Théodore, faithful to the program, opened his heart to his three friends, whose amazement was immense. At first, Théophraste exhaled a boundless indignation and, in atrocious terms, poured the blackest venom over all women, without exception.

They almost came to blows, and the sacred Vehm was within an inch of dissolution. Théodule was liquefied in dolor, but Théophile, secretly hungry for independence and hoping that a revolution would burst forth—but not daring to say so—maintained a bleak silence.

Nevertheless, everything calmed down; the artificial equilibrium was restored; each block, momentarily lifted up, fell heavily back into its hole; and the terrible schoolmaster Théophraste, considering that his flock was, in sum, about to be increased by one unit, ended up blossoming in the hope of a more extensive domination.

The inseparables went in a body to request, on Théodore's behalf, the hand of the unfortunate, who did not see the gulf into which she was about to be precipitated by her blind desire to espouse a descendant of gallant knights.

The hell commenced on the first day. It had been agreed that the communal life would continue. The newlyweds obtained, it is true, agreement that they would be left alone at night, but it was necessary, as before, that everyone should get up at a certain time and that no one should flinch in the observation of the most monastic rule.

Every morning, Théodore had to render an exact account of everything that he had been able to accomplish in the obscurity of the conjugal chamber, and the poor woman soon discovered, with alarm, that she had married four men.

The most frightful future unfolded before her eyes the day after her sad wedding. She saw the full extent of the base stupidity of the flashy individual whose wife she had become, and the humiliating state of slavery resulting from that imbecilic affiliation.

Her letters, and those she received, were opened by the odious Théophraste and read aloud before the other three, in her presence. The bison dropped his dung and his impure drool over the confidences of women, mothers and daughters.

With the consent of her husband, the tyranny of that abominable pedant was exercised over her clothing, her posture, her appetite, her speech, her gaze and her slightest gestures.

Stifled, trampled, kneaded, in despair, she fell into a profound silence and began to envy, with all her heart, the fortunate individuals who traveled in hearses unaccompanied by any cortege.

In the beginning, the quadrille locked her in when it went to its office, where the administration would not have permitted it to take her. Grave inconveniences forced it to relax that rigor. Then, she was free, or able to think that she was free, to come and go for about eight hours a day. She did not know that the concierge, handsomely paid, was keeping a record of her entrances and exits, and that spies stationed in the neighboring streets kept careful watch on her every move.

The prisoner, therefore, profited from this simulacrum of release to inebriate herself on an atmosphere other than that of the infamous cloister where she dared not even breathe in. She went to see her parents and old friends; she strolled along the boulevards and the quays. She was punished for it by scenes of diabolical violence and became even unhappier—for Théodore, in addition to his other charming qualities, was as jealous as a Berber Bluebeard.

It was too much. That which naturally and infallibly comes of such a regime transpired. Madame Théodore listened without displeasure to the words of a stranger, who seemed to her to be a man of genius by comparison with such idiots. She saw him as being as handsome as a God because he did not resemble them, thought him infinitely generous because he spoke to her softly, and immediately became his mistress, in an indescribable transport of joy.

What happened next has been related, in recent days, in a news item.

But I am told that, on the very night of the fall, the four men being reunited, the Demon appeared to them.

Two Phantoms

To Laurent Tailhade[1]

FEW things were as afflicting as the rupture of that friendship.

Mademoiselle Cléopâtre du Tesson des Mirabelles of Saint-Pothin-sur-le-Gland and Miss Penelope Elfrida Magpie had cherished one another for thirty winters. They had even finished up resembling one another.

The former belonged to the equine race of those unsaleable and unforgiving blue-stockings unappeased by any sacrifice. She had written twenty volumes of sociology or history and ruined an equal number of publishers therewith. There were not enough boxes along the banks of the Seine to collect the tomes that agonizing periodicals offered at a premium to their subscribers, and whose

---

1 Laurent Tailhade (1854-1919) was a Symbolist poet notorious for his Anarchist affiliations and his fondness for dueling. It was an article defending him that occasioned the chain of events leading to Bloy's dismissal from the pages of *Gil Blas*; Bloy subsequently felt hurt when he held Tailhade partly responsible for the scurrilous parody of him featured in Fernand Kolney's *roman à clef Le Salon de Madame Truphot* (1904). "Deux fantômes" was originally published in the 15 septembre issue of *Gil Blas*. Bloy's biographer Jean Steinmann claims that Penelope Magpie is a caricature of Louise Read, one of the many people with whom he had quarrelled.

scarcely-sumptuous binding made them appropriate to reward the application of schoolgirls when prizes were distributed.

The daughter of a stern translator of Homer, whose death she alone deplored, and a frightful dame barbecued by the solstices who was thought to be an old spy, that Corinne of the sarcophagi could not console herself for not having been able to espouse a famous man by whom she believed that she was adored. Having been beautiful in olden days, according to a few paleographers, she was tremulously resigned to planting the tree of philosophical liberty in the midst of her own ruins.

Always dressed in black, all the way to the tips of her fingernails, with her hair done up like a swan's nest, the rare slices of herself that an entirely British decorum permitted her to exhibit, were covered with a thick layer of dirt whose initial effluvia doubtless went back to the July Revolution.

In the face, she resembled a fried potato rolled in grated cheese. Her hands inclined one to think that she had "dug up her great-grandmother," as a Scandinavian proverb puts it.

In sum, her person exhaled the odor of the sixth-floor landing of a twentieth-rate furnished lodging-house. She was nevertheless much admired by a whole group of young Englishwomen, whose independence was assured by the breeding of livestock or the international traffic in those precious negroes who get whiter as they grow old. They came from various parts of the United Kingdom to Mademoiselle du Tesson's home in order to learn about literature and the high fashion of the great century of which she was the last and most illustrious professoress.

She considered these gracious disciples more as friends than pupils, however. Convinced, perhaps by personal experience, that the heart of a young woman is a gulf of turpitudes and crimes, she incited them to confidence, stirred them up with bizarre questions, suggestive and corrupting requests, and made herself the opener of their souls.

In exchange for the confessions for which she was avid, she offered her protection. As she had the reputation of a very superior woman, the little chicks ordinarily allowed to be drawn out, along with their own histories, the more or less violent histories of their parents and siblings.

Mademoiselle du Tesson called herself a Catholic, but did not approve of mass and spoke with a lively enthusiasm about the beauties of Protestantism.

Miss Penelope lived exclusively to ensure the happiness of others. A Scotswoman informed of the nonexistence of God, she adored all the inhabitants of the planet with an equal fervor.

One encountered her incessantly in the streets, going to carry consolation to someone or other. She could not hear mention of a catastrophe, a malady or an affliction without immediately setting forth in order to spread, over the grief-stricken or the dying, the balm of her advice and the electuary of her compassion.

She would have liked to be everywhere at once and often succeeded, by dint of diligence, in giving the illusion of ubiquity. One found her at the same hour at the bedside of someone dying, the reception of an immortal, on the stairway of an editor or journalist, in the drawing-room of some Jewess, at the reading of a will or behind the coffin of someone deceased.

In this manner, she insinuated herself penetratively into the lives of a multitude, who ended up supposing her to be indispensable to some mysterious equilibrium.

Some people even thought her an angel, but of a class of angels, it is true, not catalogued by Saint Denys the Aeropagite,[1] quartered at an infinite distance from the Throne of God, in some desolate steppe of the heavens, where rivers, lively springs and Marseilles soap are unknown.

She was, alas, a dirty angel, and I suspect that that circumstance was the little-known origin of the attraction that brought the wandering planet in question into orbit around the fixed Cléopâtre, considered as a sage star.

It would have been difficult to decide which of the two outdid the other in indecency. There was a rivalry of dirtiness, an assault of grime, an antagonism of stains and impure sediments, a competition in pulverulence, a conflict of rips and frays, a tournament of foul exhalations, musty odors, reeks and empyreumas.

Those two creatures loved one another, however, without blindness and passed judgment on one another, on every occasion with an extreme independence.

"That Penelope is really too filthy," clarioned Mademoiselle du Tesson. "It would need a dredger to clean her up."

"I can't imagine," Miss Magpie fluted in her turned, "how our dear Cléopâtre can neglect herself to that degree. It's almost as if she has resolved to inspire disgust. The administration of the sanitary services ought to send a crew out to her."

Except for that, they found one another infinitely satisfactory, and their friendship worked delightfully.

---

1 The sixth-century *Celestial Hierarchy* that classified angels into various categories was long attributed (wrongly) to St. Dionysius the Areopagite, who was also frequently confused with St. Denys. The actual identity of the neo-Platonist author in question remains unknown.

One serious matter, however, divided them. Cléopâtre wanted someone to marry her, no matter at what altar.

"So long as one is not living the 'double life,'" she said, one isn't really living. Physically, a woman without a husband is only respiring *up above*."

With great patience and an arrogance of opinion difficult to match, she developed that considerable axiom in her islanders.

Penelope declared, by contrast, that marriage was an ignominious estate and that the pretended necessity of lying with a man was an unsustainable abomination.

Those two incorrigible virgins quarreled quite frequently, therefore, on that subject—but the victory always went to the devouring Cléopâtre, who delighted in crushing the objections of her adversary. She only conceded one point to her: the evident inferiority of men—and that gave so much pleasure to Miss Magpie that the argument ended.

For better or worse, it remained a permanent given that the union of the sexes is a physiological law and that the exceedingly legitimate horror of distinguished women for that hideous coupling is only insurmountable in appearance.

"Women lack literature," concluded the doctress, energetically, "and marriage is the only means of making it. At random! And too bad if it shoves men aside."

One day, unknown to her friend, Cléopâtre founded a matrimonial agency—a very discreet little agency that only waved the firebrand of its offers in periodicals of an irreproachable correctness.

An anonymous prospectus on pink paper informed interested parties that the Guardian Angel of the Hearth only undertook "love-matches." It refused to get involved in financial machinations, or to offer dubious virginities, or to dangle the sparkling grape-clusters and girandoles of millions before the eyes of adventurers.

No, the Guardian Angel had assumed, as an exclusive mission, that of bringing together "elite hearts" that would otherwise never have known one another, of facilitating encounters and negotiations of guaranteed innocence. It beat the drum on behalf of unknown candors, shaded lilies, pure and bruised souls that the world does not understand—only lent itself, in conclusion, to completely and absolutely irreproachable alliances.

That noble enterprise had some success. Aging purities trembling with hope emerged from their lairs and ran to empty their savings into Cléopâtre's hands.

A very austere Genevan schoolmistress and an extremely affable decorated gentleman received visitors of either sex and drafted the correspondence. The foundress only involved herself personally in certain difficult cases in which eloquence was necessary. She then asked people to address her as Madame Aristide.

One day, around "the time when everything is in love and everything pullulates," Penelope—yes, Penelope—presented herself, also demanding the ideal spouse.

I was not there, unfortunately, but it appeared that these demands were excessive, and that Madame Aristide's intervention was required.

What an encounter, and what a scene! Cléopâtre being enraged by the unveiling of her anonymity, and Penelope being furious at being caught red-handed in concupiscence, their true natures suddenly emerged—their true nature as harpies, a thousand times more odious and malodorous than their bodies—and reciprocally turned themselves over one another's heads, like chamber-pots.

The Terrible Punishment of a Dentist

To Edouard d'Arbourg[1]

"WELL, Monsieur, would you do me the honor of telling me what you want?"

The person the printer was addressing could have been absolutely anyone, selected at random from the insignificant or the vacant—one of those men who give the impression of being plural, so much do they express ambiance, collectivity and wholeness. He might have been called *We*, like the Pope, and resembled an encyclical.

His face, applied with a spade, belonged to the innumerable category of clumsy southern louts, which no interbreeding can refine but in whom, however, everything—including the coarseness itself—is mere appearance.

He could not reply immediately because he was beside himself and, at that very moment, was making a desperate attempt to be someone. His large eyes, full of uncertainty, were rolling, almost jumping out of their sockets, like those balls in a game of chance that seem to hesitate

---

1 Edouard d'Arbourg was an occasional contributor to *Gil Blas*; it seems that he suggested the idea for this story to Bloy. He is the dedicatee of two further stories in the collection. "Terrible châtiment d'un dentiste" originally appeared in the 22 septembre 1893 issue of *Gil Blas*.

at the rim before falling into the numbered pocket where the destiny of an imbecile will be accomplished.

"Oh, damn it," he exclaimed, finally, in a strong Toulouse accent, "perhaps it's not God's thunder of which I've come in search to your shop. You're going to make me a hundred wedding announcements."

"Very good, Monsieur. Here are our models; you can make your choice. Does Monsieur desire a luxury printing on fine laid paper or Japanese imperial?"

"Luxury? Of course! One doesn't get married every day. I certainly don't think that you're going to run them off on toilet-paper. The most imperial that you have, that's understood. But above all, don't take it into your head to throw in a black border, for God's sake!"

The printer, a simple man from Vaugirard, who feared that he might be in the presence of a lunatic that it was necessary not to excite, contented himself with protesting mildly against the suspicion of such negligence.

When it came to drafting the copy, the client's hand trembled so forcefully that the craftsman had to write to his dictation:

> *Monsieur le docteur Alcibiade Gerbillon has the honor of informing you of his marriage to Mademoiselle Antoinette Planchard. The nuptial benediction will be given in the parish church of Aubervillers.*

Vaugirard and Aubervillers are hardly neighbors! thought the typographer, who collected his payment in advance.

Evidently, they were not neighbors. Dr. Alcibiade Gerbillon, dental surgeon, had been wandering around Paris for a good fifteen hours.

All the other steps relative to his marriage, which was to take place in two days, he had accomplished calmly, in the manner of a somnambulist. Only that formality of the circular had upset him. This is why.

Gerbillon was a murderer deprived of sleep.

Explain that if you can. Having perpetrated his crime in the most cowardly and ignoble fashion, but without any emotion, like the brute he was, remorse had only commenced for him with the arrival of a printed missive, broadly framed in black, by means of which an entire family in mourning begged him to attend his victim's funeral.

That typographical masterpiece had distressed, disturbed and doomed him. He pulled out perfectly good teeth, clumsily gold-plated negligible stumps, harassed precious gums, loosened jaws that time had respected, and inflicted entirely new tortures upon his clientele.

His solitary odontechnician's bed was visited by somber nightmares, in which even the vulcanized rubber dentures that he had personally placed in the mouths of distraught citizens who honored him with their confidence were grinding.

And the exclusive cause of that trouble was the banal message that had so calmly welcomed all the patented notables of the locality—Alcibiade being one of those adorers of the Moloch of Imbeciles for whom print is unforgiving.

Would you believe it? He had committed murder—actually committed murder—*for love*.

Justice doubtless desires that such a crime should be imputed to the dentist's reading-matter, which was the sole aliment of the murderer's brain. By virtue of seeing amorous situations reach tragic denouements in serial novels, he had allowed himself gradually to be overcome by the temptation to dispose, at a stroke, of the umbrella-merchant who formed an obstacle to his happiness.

That young and superbly-toothed individual, whose jaws he had never had any opportunity to devastate, had been on the point of marrying Antoinettte, the daughter of the wealthy ironmonger Planchard, for whom Gerbillon had burned silently since the day when, after he had broken a tubercular molar, the charming girl had fainted in his arms.

The banns were about to be published. With the rapid decisiveness that makes dentists so redoubtable, Alcibiade had plotted the extermination of his rival.

One the morning of a torrential downpour, the umbrella-merchant had been found dead in his bed. Medical examination rendered it manifest that a villain of the most dangerous species had strangled the poor fellow in his sleep.

The diabolical Gerbillon, who knew better than anyone what had happened, confirmed that opinion audaciously and honored himself with an implacable logic in the scientific demonstration of the crime. His precautions, moreover, had been so well taken that after an investigation as vain as it was meticulous, the law was obliged to renounce discovering the guilty party.

The sanguinary dentist was therefore saved, but not unpunished, as you shall see. As he intended that his crime should profit him, the umbrella-merchant was hardly underground before he began to lay siege to Antoinette.

The superior attitude that he had shown in the course of the investigation, the light with which he had inundated that obscure drama, and, finally, the respectful urgency of his delicate compassion for a young person so cruelly afflicted, facilitated his access to her heart.

It was not, to tell the truth, a difficult heart to capture, a Babylon of a heart. The ironmonger's daughter was a reasonable and healthy virgin who only sank into her dolor to a limited depth. She laid no claim to the vainglory of eternal lamentations, nor did she set out to be inconsolable.

"One does not live for the dead . . . one husband lost, ten found . . . etc.," Alcibiade murmured to her. A few sentences extracted from the same gulf soon unveiled to her the nobility of the extractor, who seemed to her to be transcendent.

"It's your heart, Mademoiselle, that I would like to uproot," he said to her one day. It was a decisive remark.

That charming speech, which the young woman's education fortunately permitted her to savor, made up her mind. Gerbillon was, in any case, an eligible spouse. An understanding was easily reached and the marriage made.

Why should a happiness so dearly conquered be poisoned by the memory of death? Had not the famous letter of mourning, whose impression was beginning to fade, reappeared in the imagination of the murderer, who had stupidly believed himself to be denounced by it? On the eve of his marriage—as we have just seen—the obsession had returned more forcefully, driving him to the brink of madness, causing him to wander for an entire day, like a fugitive, in Paris, where he was not resident, until he terrible moment when he had finally plucked up the courage to order his wedding announcements from that printer in Vaugirard, who had surely divined his crime.

It was hardly worth the trouble of having been so clever, so clear-sighted and to have put the law off the track so completely and to have, against all hope, obtained the hand of a woman he idolized, only to arrive at the misery of being pestered by hallucinations!

The intoxication of the early days was only a respite. The delicate crescent-horns of the newly-weds' honey-moon had not yet ceased to prick the azure when a seed of tribulation materialized.

One morning, Alcibiade discovered a picture of the umbrella-merchant. Oh, it was a simple photograph that Antoinette had innocently accepted from him when she thought she was on the brink of marrying him.

The dentist, carried away by fury, immediately tore it up before the eyes of his wife, who was revolted by that violence, even though the relic did not seem to her to be very precious.

At the same time, however—because it is impossible to destroy anything whatsoever—the hostile image that had only existed previously on paper, as the visible reflection of one of those fragments of the unspeakable photographic Print by which the world is enveloped, was fixed in the suddenly-impressed memory of Madame Gerbillon. Haunted, from then on, by the dead man whose memory had become almost indifferent to her, she no longer saw anything but him: saw him incessantly, breathed him in and out through her every pore, saturating her poor husband with all her effluvia—who was, in his turn, surprised and despairing at finding the cadaver between them.

After a year, they had an epileptic child, a monstrous male child who had the face of a man of thirty and bore a prodigious resemblance to the man that Gerbillon had murdered.

The father fled, uttering screams, wandered like a mad-man for three days, and on the evening of the fourth, sobbing as he leaned over his son's cradle, strangled him.

Alain Chartier's Reawakening[1]

To Rachilde[2]

*M*Y *dear friend, come this evening at eleven
o'clock. The door to the garden will be ajar.
You will only have to push it gently. I'll be waiting for
you under the arbor. My husband has gone away for
two days, and has taken the dog. If I lose everything,
too bad. I love you and I want to be yours.*

Rolande

On receiving this note, young Duputois went so pale
that his colleagues thought some catastrophe had occurred.
Being very discreet, he scrupulously stuffed the message in

1 Alain Chartier (1385-1430) was a poet who was sent as an ambassador to Scotland to negotiate a marriage between Margaret, the daughter of James I, and the dauphin who subsequently reigned as Louis
XI. An apocryphal story invented long after his death related that,
in spite of his legendary ugliness, Margaret once kissed Chartier as a
testament to his poetic gift. "Le Réveil d'Alain Chartier" was originally
published in the 29 septembre 1893 issue of *Gil Blas*.
2 Rachilde (Marguerite d'Eymery, 1860-1953), who married Alfred
Vallette, the co-founder and editor of the *Mercure de France*, was one of
the central figures in the Decadent Movement, and one of the principal shapers of its image in such novels as *Monsieur Vénus* (1884) and
La Marquise de Sade (1981).

the most mysterious corner of his wallet and stammered something about a threat from a creditor.

It was, however, impossible for him to go back to work. Reading those few lines had shattered him. He experienced the physical malaise of a man who has not eaten for two days: empty head, dolorous articulations and feverishness. He had a firebrand in the hollow of his stomach, an intolerable heartbeat and a hysterical lump in his throat.

It is a banal observation that the disturbance of love procures in young people, and even in old ones, the sensations of a condemned man who is being dragged to the guillotine. There is such a connection between execution and sensuality that in certain towns in the Middle Ages, the aldermen or mayor demanded that the executioner's lair should be relegated to the low streets where prostitution was located. The lechers of the "tall tree," as Panurge put it, must sometimes have mistaken it.

Florimond Duputois was not young enough to practice psychology. He was already some years past twenty and gave no thought to self-analysis. He merely observed that the skin of his cranium was hurting and that his legs were unsteady. Having tried to drink it several times, the water of the administrative carafe seemed to him to have an aftertaste of carrion.

Why that letter? he said to himself. *I haven't done anything, after all, to seduce that lovely woman. I've only spoken to her in private twice, at the most, and I'm sure that she must take me for an idiot. It's true that I'm no more disgusting than anyone else, especially when I recite verses after dinner. I can even well imagine that a woman might, at that moment, take a fancy to me, even be infatuated. My God yes, why not? All the same, though, that letter's a bit stiff and I think the rendezvous is lacking too many preliminaries.*

He moralized all day, remonstrating with himself very sagely, for the young man nourished himself exclusively on the roots of virtue.

The husband was an old friend of his family, who had given him useful protection. He owed his employment at he ministry to him, the promise of a brilliant future, a considerable number of agreeable connections, and dined at his home several times a month. He could not cuckold the man without plunging head first into a pit of filth. That would be certain, absolute dishonor, the most base and fetid action, a treason such that one could never hold up one's head again . . . etc.

In consequence, he took the generous resolution to be punctual at the rendezvous.

Yes, certainly, he would go, and find out what was at the bottom of it. He would talk to her about the dire fate of an inconsiderate spouse who was not hesitating to sacrifice her honor to him. He would make her sense the enormity of her sin and the frightful inconveniences of such a dangerous liaison.

Finally, he would return her to her husband, throw her back into the ever-open arms of that good man, who would never know that he had been on the brink of being subjected to the ultimate outrage.

He soon excited himself with the thought of thus recognizing the benevolence of his protector.

Oh, she had been lucky, the dear creature, to fall upon him! She might just as easily have surrendered herself to some imbecile or boor who would not have failed to abuse her, to wither the wilting flower that was so badly in need of support, of reanimation. . . .

How many others, in his place, would not have seen this as an opportunity to satisfy their vile instincts, to triumph in their turkey-cock vanity, and would doubtless already be shouting from the rooftops the fall of a unfortunate gone astray, a victim of her enthusiasm!

I have forgotten to mention that Florimond Duputois had a bulbous nose, eyes like soup-spoons, a mouth like a lepidopteran sucker, granular skin, a sagging rump and a great fear of cows. I will add that he belonged to the symbolist constellation, and that he was an assiduous contributor to the *Grimoire*, the *Mélusine* and the *Revue de Crotales*.[1]

He escaped from his office a little before time, ran to a hairdresser to have himself adonized, had a palingenetic dinner, reread a few pages of "L'Après-midi d'un faune" with the aim of elevating his heart, and, sure of himself, finally caught the omnibus to Auteuil.

The door to Madame Rolande's garden was indeed ajar. Pushed by him with infinite precaution, it gradually yawned upon a black gulf. The path, scarcely visible near the threshold, disappeared immediately in the depths of the bushes. Having often been admitted to that labyrinth to seek inspiration while strolling, however, he knew, as they say, every twist and turn.

Closing the door behind him, therefore, he advanced at a processional pace, recovered from all his disturbance, the big bell of his heart ringing full tilt.

The silence was as profound as any malefactor could have desired or dreaded in that sedative quarter inhabited by invalids or exceedingly precious millionaires. Only a

---

1 A *crotale* is a rattlesnake. A *grimoire*, in this context, is an unintelligible document.

few vague rumors were audible in the distance, in the direction of the Point-du-Jour, and the prolonged plaint of one of those melancholy dogs in Maldoror that torment the infinite.

As he drew closer to the arbor of birthwort and honeysuckle where the guilty spouse was waiting, his assurance diminished, his stride became more uncertain and his tremulousness more irrepressible. In the end, his teeth were chattering so forcefully that he was afraid of waking up the little birds, and sensed that he was so pale that he wondered whether he might be about to taint the leaves with his pallor, like a phosphorescent fish.

Suddenly, a hand was placed on his shoulder.

"I'm here my love," said Madame Rolande's voice—and almost immediately, the two arms of that uninhibited woman were wrapped around his neck, while a life-or-death kiss ate away at his soul.

Oh, the voracity there was in that wild kiss! The young man had anticipated everything, except that impetuous, unappeasable, eternal kiss: that odorant and intoxicating kiss through which passed the ferocious perfumes of Fleurs du Mal, the unsettling volatilities of Venison and the execrable peppers of Desire; the kiss that had claws like an eagle and went hunting like a lion, which entered into him like a sword of fire and filled his ears with the bellowing of rams or mountain goats; that frightful kiss of opium, furious folly, brutalization and ecstasy!

The chaste intentions had decamped. They had gone to the Devil, to God's thunder, or into the bottom of a lunar creek, along with the harangues or Orphic abjurations previously elaborated.

Duputois was falling into the abyss when a sound of footsteps became audible. The darkness being absolute, it was impossible to make out anything at all. The lyricist of the *Revue des Crotales* then received, full in the face, the thrust of two furious hands, which shoved him away and almost made him fall to the ground.

Madame Rolande, having got rid of the poor devil, had leapt backwards, and now he could hear the whispers of two people rapidly drawing away toward the house.

Hardly daring to breathe, and not daring to move, he remained motionless in the darkness, hoping for he knew not what.

Finally, however, exhausted by fatigue and frozen by the stars, he went back to the garden door, still ajar, and found himself on the sound sidewalk of the downcast, having made no more noise than a black ant emigrating in the black night, as discomfited and bowed down as an adolescent full of soliloquies and prosody can be.

The next day, someone asked for him in the antechamber of his ministry. He found himself in the presence of a very handsome man, sufficiently athletic, who gave the impression of a cavalry officer of the most exquisite politeness, and who spoke in these terms:

"Monsieur, yesterday, a confusion of envelopes placed a note from a woman that was intended for me in your hands. There is no need, I think, to remind you of the content of that message. I implore you, in fact, carefully to forget it. On receiving, for my part, the few lines that should have reached you, I fortunately divined the substitution of addresses, and arrived just in time to avert the deadly consequences. You are known to be a gallant man, and I am counting on you, in exchange for the letter I have here, immediately to return the one that belongs to me. I will add—quite needlessly, to be sure, Monsieur Poet— that *Caesar's wife must be above suspicion.*"

That final only-too-clear phrase was emphasized in such a significant fashion that the weakling, incapable of expectorating a diphthong, did as he was asked.

This is what the other letter contained:

> *Monsieur Duputois, I would be infinitely obliged to you if, in future, you would spare me the honor of your dedications in the petty revues. Your poems are incontestably delightful, but I confess my preference for humble prose, and the role of muse does not suit me.*
>
> *Agreeably, etc.*

That insignificant adventure occurred in 187*. Florimond Duputois, increasingly protected, is continuing his stint at the ministry. It seems certain that he will be promoted to Chévalier[1] next fourteenth of July.

---

1 Of the *Légion d'honneur.*

The Obliging Stroker[1]

To Remy de Gourmont[2]

I KNEW him in 1864, when he was scarcely an adolescent. We lived together for more than twenty years and I loved him as one rarely loves a brother.

Today, when the unfortunate has descended to somewhat below the level of the dead, I can certainly say that in his regard I was the most diligent, the most attentive and the most devoted educator.

All the good that was in his poor soul—as deprived now as the granaries of the Famine—he received from my mouth, as the children of the nocturnal eagles that frighten the night are nourished.

---

1 *Frotteur*, which I have rendered as "stroker," by virtue of its inherent reference to friction, is used trivially to refer to a floor-polisher or some similar domestic appliance, but it is also employed in a sexual context, in both slang and medical terminology, the latter with respect to the technically-defined act of *frottage*. "Le Frotteur compatissant" was originally published in the 6 octobre 1893 issue of *Gil Blas*. Jean Steinmann claims that Thierry is based on one of Bloy's oldest friends, Georges Landry.

2 Remy de Gourmont (1858-1915) was the principal critic associated with the Decadent/Symbolist Movement and one of its most elegant exemplars, especially in his short fiction and prose-poetry. He was one of the co-founders, with Alfred Vallette, of the Symbolist *Mercure de France*.

I borrowed from the altar-lamp, the lamp that is never extinguished, the tranquil and upright flame that was necessary to remove the obstructions from an intelligence naturally elaborative of darkness.

Being the elder, I took him on my shoulders and, for a third of my sad life, I carried him in the roseate light of horizons, separating him a little more every day from miry levels, while I grew up myself, and I was never bowed down by that burden.

I would have had a horror of complaining, though. I was so sure of having snatched a prey from the Demon of Stupidity, a prey all the more precious because it seemed to have been claimed in advance, by virtue of its origin, to that Captor of the multitude.

Némorin Thierry had been harvested from a low branch of that medlar-tree of the Bourgeoisie whose fruits rot as soon as they touch the ground. He obtained, therefore, from his parents, a mind wide open to mediocre ideas and resistant to any impression of a superior order.

It was a pedagogy more than difficult, a continual feat of strength: it was necessary to block the funnel with one hand and lubricate the narrow conduits with the other, to clear the ground of weeds and graft the wild root, rid it of caterpillars and layer it, all at the same time.

It was indispensable to remove that poor wretch from himself, to sift and filter him, to inaugurate him, in sum, to condition him, in a sense, a more lively little phantom that would gradually decant his identity.

The results were such, in appearance, that it is excusable for me to have been able to consider myself a thaumaturge, to the point of forgetting the formal law of regression to their rudimentary time that applies to all animals and vegetable whose cultivation is interrupted.

I had the misfortune of not paying heed to the incessant reminders of the primordial and unfailing dog-rose. I believed, in a word, that poor Némorin could walk unaided, and, having carried him for twenty years, I committed the irreparable imprudence of setting him down.

What has become of him, I do not know whether I shall have the strength to say, but how could I suppose that so much effort would be so stupidly, so completely, so abominably wasted, from the very outset, and would have no other reward than the infinite bitterness of observing the ultimate futility?

He was known as gentle Thierry, and that was not an antiphrasis. He was as gentle as the down-feathers of doves, as gentle as holy oils, as gentle as moonlight. Let no one suspect me of exaggeration here. He really was so gentle that one could not imagine an individual belonging to the male sex, and, in consequence, summoned to the reproduction of the species, who could be any more so.

He melted in the hand like chocolate, assuaging the ambiance, making one think of the silkiest of cocoons. Nothing was capable of making him angry, of exciting his indignation, and it was the despair of an educator determined to virilize the void never to obtain the palest flash, no matter how furiously that gelatinous consciousness was stirred and poked.

Several times I tried to reassure myself by supposing one of those natures that I ask permission to name eucharistic—"steeped in ambrosia and honey," as Chénier[1] put it—the strength of which consists precisely in enduring everything, and which seem to be placed in the human turmoil in order to deaden collisions and falls. But that state

1 The poet André Chenier (1762-1794), a victim of the Terror.

of being is only presumable when accompanied by theological predestination, and unfortunately—as I recognized too late—certain appetites or obscure inclinations absolutely set aside the hypothesis of "elect clay," for which my tutorial simplicity settled.

The gentle Thierry as simply a little pig, and belonged to the dominating race of obliging strokers.

When did he begin to stroke and to be obliging? In what April of baneful germination did that bifid penchant suddenly sprout? God alone knows. Even He probably would not have cared to say, when He appeared to be capable of speaking and articulating genuinely human sounds.

What I do know is that one day, Thierry found himself completely equipped for the function. Omnibus stops, creameries patronized by little seamstresses, the vestibules of railway stations and even churches were his hippodromes of choice.

Penetrated by the idea that he absolutely had to have companionship, he wanted it above all to be simple, and from then on, by a consequence as necessary as the planetary orbits, the albumen of his ancestors rigorously demanded that sentimental vulgarity was always the choice of his heart.

Horrible simpering soilings appeared as indecomposable to him as the light of the Empyrean, but the number of them was so great that he could never succeed in fixing his spiritual love. A Don Juan of mature errand-girls and galvanoplastic seamstresses in the need of protectors, he searched assiduously for the ideal Object in the midst of crowds.

With a marvelous patience that no fiasco disconcerted, he strove to discover the tender weeper on whose bosom he might pose, like a bunch of mimosas, his bald forehead full of amnesties.

Scantily endowed in the physiological sense, he reproved the vivid pulsations of amour and doubtless only demanded inferior joys very rarely. What inebriated him, delighted him, convulsed him, shook up his soul with delights and spread throughout his being the benzoin or oliban of blissful languor was *scarcely to touch*, to palpate with infinite delicacy, to parade his tactile apparatus hither and yon, like the wingtips of a zephyr, exhaling in the meantime melodious and pitiful groans regarding the sad fate of lilies or limp bindweed trampled underfoot by the indelicacy of adventurers of lechery.

Such a beautiful constancy had to be rewarded. Beatrix appeared one day to the itinerant of the heavens.

You can laugh as much as you want, but that was how it was. She really was called Beatrix and she plied a sewing-machine.

Némorin met her in a cheap restaurant and stroked her untiringly for seven years. His entrails, it is true, often opened, even then, to intercalary calamities solicited his pizzicato, but it was not permissible for him to confine his vocation so completely.

Beatrix, for her part, did not appear to have any thirst to confiscate him, and even attempted, every spring and every autumn, to break up with the lachrymose fiddler who clung to her perennially. It did not matter; she was, even so, the Ideal, and death alone could deliver her.

How many times, when I tried yet again to get a grip on him—how many times, just Heaven, and with what sky-bathed eyes!—did he talk to me about her as the first Christians spoke of their God under the teeth of the lions!

Finally, I repeat, that liturgy of small frissons and slow sights permitted the Earth to roll round the sun seven times.

"Is she at least your mistress?" I sometimes asked him: a brutal question, I agree, which immediately made him climb back up into his stained-glass window. His negative response expired in a pious gesture.

Do I need to say it? Beatrix's mouth reeked, and so, I think, did her large feet. She was such a turkey-hen that one sensed wattles growing after a quarter of an hour of conversation. Her manners fitted her face, which one might have thought hauled out of the pickling-bucket of a low-class pork-butcher. Shrewish enough, to boot, to make a bitch abort, and as prudish as arithmetic, she welcomed into her exceedingly pure bed, without too much acrimony, the crepuscular suffrages of a few exhausted rams of petty commerce.

Gentle Thierry had to resign himself, six times out of ten, while shedding tears, to finding the door closed. Sometimes he was nearly knocked down the stairs, under a deluge of the filthiest curses. These acts of violence, which saddened him, appeared to him nevertheless to derive from an utterly divine soul, and naturally quadrupled his fervor.

"She has suffered so much!" he said, raising his conjoined hands to take heaven for his witness.

Beatrix, moreover, perceived dinners or little gifts as the privilege of that worship, and always clarified the situation admirably the following day. That scraping of femininity made him swallow five hundred times—doubtless in another style, but with what facility!—the famous words of the dazzling Courtesan: "Oh, you no longer love me! You believe what you see and not what I tell you!"

Némorin himself, in the sublime leap of his faith, came up with words that confused me: "She's explained everything!" he told me, one day, having perceived, a few hours before, in his beloved's home, a pair of men's slippers and a rack full of mostly-seasoned pipes—much more, doubtless, than the place would have led one to suppose. "She's explained everything!"

But now? Now, it is death that is stroking, and dirty death, I can assure you. It's the ignoble death that asks for no sympathy and never offers it to anyone. It's the liquid Death. . . .

My God! My God! And yet I have held him in my arms, that child of Nothing, that son of Nonexistence, that twin of Insignificance and Illusion, from which I hoped to form a living being!

I have attempted to inspire him with my soul. I have toiled, suffered, prayed, cried and sobbed for him, for years—the dearest and most precious of life. I have taken upon myself the frightful pains that he would not have had the strength to bear. Everything that a man can do, I truly believe that I have done.

In order that he should be armed against the assignations of oblivion, I have paraded and unrolled before him the images that nothing effaces; I have exterminated myself to design for him an optical illusion of realities that can never end . . . and I have not even succeeded in realizing a rogue.

Today, he is asking, imbecilically, from morn until night, that no cross should be planted on his tomb, and it is necessary to support his lower lip when one feeds him with a little pewter spoon.

The Monsieur's Past

To Eugene Demolder[1]

Penetrate, my heart,
into the charming past.
Victor Hugo

"EIGHTY THOUSAND FRANCS, Monsieur! You're not tedious. And you've traveled a hundred leagues, just like that, in order to ask me for them? You thought that I wouldn't hesitate for a moment to deprive my wife and my children of all I have, in order to pay for the extravagances of that little minx, whom I no longer recognize as my nice—whom I disown, you hear! Decidedly, you must take me for a fool. Eighty thousand francs! Why not a million while you're at it?"

These reasonable words were spoken to me fifteen years ago by a fat vine-grower in the Charente-Inférieure, whose broad face resembled a baboon's backside.

I cannot say that I had had much confidence in going to find the rich wine-merchant, previously unknown

---

1 The Belgian novelist Eugene Demolder (1862-1919) was part of the *Jeune Belgique* circle of Symbolists. "Le Passé du monsieur" was originally published in the 20 octobre 1893 issue of *Gil Blas*.

to me. I was too familiar with the proverbial destitution of millionaires and their atrocious bad luck ever to permit myself to believe that the slightest fraction of their wealth might be disposable at the precise moment one implores them.

Nevertheless, the very enormity of the sum to be obtained had caused me to hope, at least, for some consideration. At the first glance, however, I had had a presentiment of my fatal lack of success and had only taken the step to liberate my conscience—a step, it is true, of the most singular kind. It was a matter of putting into the barrel a specific quantity of familial disinterest equivalent to the tenth part of a million, and I was surely the most ill-equipped ambassador for that kind of negotiation.

"My God, Monsieur!" I relied, "You really are too kind not to set your dogs on me immediately or end for the gendarmes. That encourages me to remind you that I'm acting on behalf of a dead woman—which is to say, in obedience to the last wishes of an unfortunate young woman who was buried two days ago. I am, as you have certainly deduced, merely a benevolent delegate who has put himself out considerably. You are perfectly free to do nothing and even to disown, as much as you lease, your own blood—but I'm very tired from my journey and I'm astonished that you have not yet made the slightest demonstration of hospitality."

These last words, intended to prolong the conversation for a few hours, during which I would strive to enlace my host, did not displease him. He softened, even becoming quite cordial, and invited me to lunch.

But, mood-lightening and suggestive as the viticultural-ist's table was, my diplomatic subtlety and my tenderizing eloquence proved ineffective, as I had anticipated, and I only took away from the visit one more bitter confirmation of my impotence to penetrate the hide of hippopotamuses or pachydermatous philosophers.

The story of the niece is perhaps the most extraordinary of all the lamentable ones I have known. Her name was Justine D*** and she died at the age of twenty-eight in the most horrible despair.

A third of that overly long existence was exclusively and vainly employed in the conquest of a poor man judged by her to be superior, whom she adored to the extent of crime and whose wife she wanted to become at any price. Our meager and twisted *fin-de-siècle*, like a pig's tail, must offer few examples of such bewitchment.

The miracle is that that flower of passion, that passiflora of amour, had grown in the most refractory humus, in the most unfavorable conditions one can imagine.

She was one of those production-line virgins, such as commerce in fabrics or a monopoly in pickles produces for us, engendered from the estimable loins of a businessman who had always paid his bills. Brought up, in consequence with a sage horror of constellations and aureoles, one would naturally assume that nothing would be more rectilinear than her sentiments or transports.

Her heart had been cultivated like a kitchen garden of limited extent, in which the smallest strips were calculated for the cooking-pot: no useless flowers whose frivolous brightness brings no profit; at the very most a few pansies or violets bordering the beans and salad vegetables, in order not to exile poetry completely.

Two or three unparalleled tomes by Émile Souvestre or the great Dumas, a collection of choice morsels and the daily reading of news items from the *Petit Journal* were more than enough to sate her literary tastes.

In sum, no girl ever appeared more destined to become the ornament and recompense of an "honest man."

I cannot take responsibility for explaining prodigies any more than mysteries, and you must not expect me to provide a psychological elucidation of arbitrary matters of which I happen to be the narrator.

What is certain is that the tree produced fruits that no longer permitted it to be recognized and the minuscule kitchen garden produced strange flowers, probably exotic, instead of the turnips and potatoes one expected to see emerging from the ground.

A heroine—a veritable and scandalous heroine of amour—suddenly appeared in that Justine, whom one would have thought worthy to raise herself up to be the supporting beam of some businessman. Except that, in order that nature should not lose all its rights, the man she loved, much more than her own life, was a mediocrity among mediocrities, a blond clerk who scraped a viola, daubed little water-color landscapes and conserved, at thirty, the prestige of the fluffy hair of adolescence.

That basilisk of shopgirls gave her the sublime illusion—and this is the incredible drama that ensued.

Narcisse Lépinoche—that was the vanquisher's name—did not refuse absolutely to marry Justine. As well that one as another, after all. But only having, outside of his employment, a miserly capital by way of resources, and being desirous, in addition, of casting his net for a little while longer, he did not exhibit any haste to enchain to his existence a young woman without a sou, whose beauty was by no means overwhelming.

I have never thought him sordid, but heroic disinterest was not his thing and since the expression talks of "forming a household," did not rudimentary prudence demand at least that they wait for the heritage of Uncle Tiburce, who made a hundred thousand francs a year on his stakes and would doubtless not be long in quitting a world where his beautiful soul was in exile?

Justine had, in fact, been ruined for some time by her imbecile father, who had invested his entire fortune in the drilling of the famous tunnel under the Himalayas, destined to link British India with Manchuria.

The colossal failure of that enterprise having precipitated the speculator into the most profound of abysms, the young woman lived with her mother on the miserable debris of former opulence, clinging to the hope of that fortunate heritage that was to unite her with her Lépinoche, whom she imagined to be handsomer and worthier of idolatry every day—for he was her uncle, her father's brother, that Tiburce of wines and spirits, who was known to be so rich and so miserly but who was old and childless. Once a year, by virtue of the effect of an old habit, he sent a case of bottles, and that was all. It was necessary to wait, alas, since the man could only be useful in the manner of pigs—which is to say, after his death.

Unfortunately, the skinflint did not seem to want to kick the bucket, and years went by that way. Justine, seeing herself growing old, struggled with rage, and Lépinoche, visibly disgusted, scarcely concealed his researches in other directions. He even became insolent. I do not know all the details, or the ins and outs, but it is certain that the young woman was too passionate ever to have refused anything to her wretched lover and I believe that I noticed in him more than once the ferocious deception and cowardly cruelty of a lady-killer who only has to ask for anything whatsoever and has given nothing to obtain everything.

One day, someone came in haste to see me on behalf of the unfortunate young woman, who wanted to speak to me in private before dying.

The priest, whom I encountered on the stairway, seemed glad to see me. He was very pale and affirmed that my presence would relieve him of a great weight; then he went away, begging me to be charitable.

I had only just returned from a long voyage and I had not seen Justine for some months. I scarcely recognized her, so beautiful had she become under the claws of death. I could only rediscover her eyes—what eyes!—in an entirely white face, over which shadows and flushes passed, as if a torch were being moved back and forth in front of her. Her lips, absolutely colorless, were only visible in contrast to the dark line of teeth blackened by fever. All the rest was indistinct, unified, melted into that almost radiant, almost luminous whiteness: a block of polished alabaster reflecting a carpet of snow! Her hair had disappeared in an ample bonnet.

I am sure that I felt nothing at the time but pity, the most heart-rending pity of my life, especially when she spoke to me. It was only later that I was to sense the supernatural beauty of that configuration of Terror and Pain.

She made an effort to sit up in her bed.

"Monsieur," she said, in a very low voice, "I've just received extreme unction, and am going to die. God is good, and I hope that he won't reject me. I asked you to come because you're a true friend and you will, I'm certain, do what a desolate heart humbly asks of you.

85

"No one, except the priest who has just left, knows as yet what I've done. When I'm dead, everyone will know, and there will be horrible shame. . . .

"I've ruined several people who had confidence in me and whom I've deceived odiously. For three years, my life has been nothing but an imposture, a lie, every hour of every day. I have made old friends of the family believe that my mother and I were not ruined. Large sums have been lent to me, which I have thrown into speculations, and which I have lost. Without understanding it, but with the obstinacy of a damned soul, I trafficked in shares on the Bourse . . . in the hope of making a fortune, you understand. . . .

"I wanted to become rich for the man I loved to the perdition of my soul, whom I still love and for whom I'm dying . . . uselessly!

"I have robbed poor people. Once, Monsieur, I robbed an old woman, infirm and almost blind, of a few bonds and obligations that were all she had, and I replaced them with advertisements on colored paper. That Christian woman, who cherished me, will be forced to beg for her bread. As I lost continually, I lent myself to any and all crimes in the illusion of recovering my losses.

"In short, I owe more than eighty thousand francs. Only my uncle can repay them—my rich uncle, whose death I've so often desired. Go and find him, I beg you, as soon as I've been put in the earth, and tell him that it's me who has died, and that I died terrified of all those maledictions upon my poor grave. Terrified!"

The dying woman uttered a loud scream and, throwing her arms around my neck, howled these final words, which I can still hear:

"Oh, if you knew. . . if you knew what I can see!"

That was the end. I was forced to disentangle myself from the cadaver, whose fingernails were digging into my flesh and whose eyes, incredibly dilated, were still gazing. . . .

The uncle, naturally, paid nothing.

Lépinoche, to whom I related that death a short while afterwards, admitted to me that he really found it all quite sad. Four years later, he married the daughter of a high-class flunkey, an honest woman, who disapproves of all insanities and no longer permits him to associate with me.

"Whatever You Want!"

To Prince Alexandre Ourousof[1]

MAXENCE, fatigued by a long evening of pleasure, arrived at the corner of the street and the Ruelle Dupleix, opposite the École Militaire. That night, at one o'clock in the morning, the location, which was merely wretched in broad daylight, had something sinister about it. The black alleyway, most of all, was not reassuring. That muddy stretch, where artillerymen and cavalrymen are lodged for next to nothing in frightful rooming-houses, made the nocturnal pedestrian anxious.

He deliberated, however. A rumor was audible in the Boulevard de Grenelle, avoided by the wise, and the horror of falling into a drunken brawl inclined him to choose the filthy trench, at the extremity of which he thought he was sure to find a more peaceful vale for the course of his amorous dreams. He had emerged from the arms of his mistress and felt the need to nurse his lechery in the somnolence of a disturbance-free return.

---

1 Prince Alexandre Ourousof arrived in Paris from Moscow in 1891—in order, according to Bloy's journals, to rally to Bloy's defence in his quarrel with Joséphin Péladan. He published a commemorative volume of texts related to *Les Fleurs du Mal*, entitled *Le Tombeau de Charles Baudelaire* (1896). "Tout ce que tu voudras" was originally published in the 27 octobre 1893 issue of *Gil Blas*.

"Well, have you decided—yes or no?" said an abject voice, striving to make itself amiable.

Maxence then saw a fat woman detach herself from the nearest wall, who came to offer him the commodity of her amour.

"I won't cost you much, and I'll do whatever you want, darling."

She was reciting a formula, but the immobile roamer listened to it as he would have listened to his own heart beating. It was stupid, and he could not have said why, but that voice stirred him. He could not have explained it, the poor man, if it had been a matter of saving his life.

His disturbance was, however, quite certain—and that disturbance became an intolerable anguish when he sensed his soul going adrift on that ignominious offer, which bore him like an ebb-tide toward the most distant reaches of his past: memories of a marvelous sweetness, which that manner of reappearance profaned unspeakably!

The impressions of his childhood had been something divine, and his present life, alas, had nothing glorious about it.

When he tried to recuperate, by evoking them after some spree, they came to him simply and faithfully, those impressions, like chilly and abandoned ewes who asked for nothing better than always to follow their shepherd . . . but this time he had not summoned them. They had come of their own accord, or, rather, it was another voice that had called them, a voice that was doubtless heeded, as was his own—which was abominable, and incomprehensible.

"Whatever you want. I'll do whatever you want, my treasure. . . ."

No, truly, it was intolerable. His mother was dead, burned alive in a fire. He remembered a charred hand, the only part of the cadaver they dared to show him.

His only sister, five years his elder, who had brought him up with so much solicitude, and to whom he owed all that was best in him, had ended her life in a no less tragic manner. The ocean had swallowed her, with fifty other passengers, in a much-publicized shipwreck off one of the most inhospitable coasts of the Bay of Gascony. It had not been possible to recover her body.

And those two dolorous creatures possessed him every time he leaned his elbows on the parapet of his memory, watching his own life flow by.

Oh well! It was horrible, and it was monstrous, but the whore who was standing there, on that sidewalk—on that quay of hell, as Maeterlinck put it—had exactly the same voice as his sister, that creature of election who had seemed to him to belong to the angelic hierarchies and whose feet, he believed, would have purified the mud of Sodom.

Oh, undoubtedly, it was her voice—inexpressibly degraded, fallen from the havens, rolled in the filthy gulfs where the thunder dies—but her voice, all the same, to the point at which he was tempted to flee, screaming and sobbing.

Was it true, then, that the dead can slip in that way into the company of those who are living, or who put on a semblance of being alive?

At the very moment when the aged prostitute promised him her execrable flesh—and in what style, just heavens!—he heard his sister, eaten by the fish a quarter of a century ago, recommending him to love God and love the poor.

"If you knew what beautiful thighs I have!" said the vampire.

"If you knew how beautiful Jesus is!" said the saint.

"Come home with me, then, you naughty boy; I have a nice fire and a nice bed. You'll see that you won't have any regrets," continued the one.

"Don't cause your guardian angel grief," murmured the other.

Involuntarily, he pronounced that pious recommendation, which had filled his childhood, out loud.

Those words gave the solicitor a shock and she started to tremble. Raising her head to look at him with her old, liquid, bloodshot eyes—extinct mirrors that seemed to have reflected all the images of debauchery and all the images of torture—she looked at him avidly, with the frightful gaze of a drowning victim contemplating, one last time, the glaucous sky, through the wisdom of water asphyxiating her. . . .

There was a moment's silence.

"I beg your pardon, Monsieur," she said, finally. "I was wrong to speak to you. I'm just an old camel, a mattress for lechers, and you ought to have kicked me into the gutter. Go home, and may the Lord protect you."

Maxence, confounded, immediately saw her plunge into darkness.

She was right, after all; he had to go home. The laggard headed, therefore, toward the Boulevard de Grenelle—but how slowly! That encounter had literally stunned him.

He had not taken ten steps when the old cannibal reappeared, running after him.

"Monsieur, I beg you, don't go that way."

"Why shouldn't I go that way?" he asked. "It's my route, since I live in Vaugirard."

"Too bad—you have to go back, make a detour, even if you have to walk for an extra hour. You're risking being knocked over the head as you cross the boulevard. If you must know, half the pimps in Paris are meeting there on business. They're strung out all the way from the abattoirs to the tobacco factory. The police are leaving them to it. You won't have anyone to protect you and you'll certainly come to harm."

Maxence was tempted to reply that he had no need of being protected, but fortunately, he sensed the stupidity of such bravado.

"All right," he said. "I'll go back toward the Invalides. It's a bit much, all the same. I'm worn out, and the extra distance is exasperating. They ought to send the cavalry after those pimps. . . ."

"Perhaps there's another way," said the old woman, after a momentary hesitation.

"Ah! Let's hear it."

Very humbly, then, she explained that being well-known in that fine society, it would be easy for her to get someone through. . . .

"Except," she added, with surprising softness, "that it would be necessary for them to believe that you're an . . . acquaintance—and for that, it would be indispensable to let me take your arm."

Maxence hesitated in his turn, fearing a trap. But an unknown force acted within him; his hesitation was brief . . . and he was able to pass through the filthy crowd without insult, having that creature on his arm and close to his heart, who was congratulated as she passed by several bandits, and who was truly enough to discourage Sin itself.

Not a word, however, was exchanged between them. He only noticed that she squeezed his arm and pressed herself against him far more than was strictly demanded by the situation, and even that there was something convulsive in that grip.

The extraordinary disturbance that he had felt had dissipated now that she was no longer speaking. It was natural to suppose it a sort of hallucination, for everyone knows how convenient that precious word is, by means of which all obscure sentiments and presentiments are elucidated.

When the time came to separate, Maxence constructed some banal formula of thanks and took out his purse with the intention of compensating the strange silent companion who might perhaps have just saved his life.

She stopped him with a gesture, though. "No, Monsieur, it's not that."

It was only then that he saw that she was weeping, for he had not dared to look at her during the half-hour they had been walking together.

"What's the matter?" he said, quite distressed, "And what can I do for you?"

"If you would care to permit me to kiss you," she replied, "it would be the great joy of my life, of my disgusting life, and it seems to me that, after that, I'd have the strength to die."

Seeing that he consented to it, she leapt upon him, groaning with love, and gave him a devouring kiss.

A plaint from the man she was stifling disentangled her.

"Adieu, Maxence," she cried, "my little Maxence, my poor brother, adieu forever, and forgive me. Now I can die."

Before her brother had time to make the slightest movement, her head was broken under the wheel of a nocturnal truck that was passing like a tempest.

Maxence no longer has a mistress. At this moment he is finishing his novitiate at the monastery of the Great Charterhouse.

The Last Firing

To Alfred Vallette[1]

When one's dead,
it's for a long time.
     An heir.

MONSIEUR FIACRE PRÉTEXTAT LABALBARIE had retired from business at the age of sixty, having acquired considerable wealth in his profession as a whitener of sepulchers.

He had never disappointed his clientele and the Genevan aristocracy, which had overloaded him for a long time with its orders, had had but one cry to celebrate his exactitude and reliability. The excellence of his handiwork, certified by the suspicious English, had obtained the suffrage of Belgium, Illinois and Michigan.

His retirement had therefore been the occasion for great regret in the two worlds, when the groans of the

---

1 Alfred Vallette (1858-1935) was the co-founder and editor of the *Mercure de France*, the pillar of the French Symbolist Movement. He published several of Bloy's books under the Mercure de France imprint, which eventually acquired the author's other copyrights in order to issue an *Oeuvres complètes* in 1963-74. "La Dernière cuite" was originally published in the 3 novembre 1863 issue of *Gil Blas*.

94

international press had announced that the famous artisan was quitting the funeral business to devote his respected white hair to cherished studies.

Fiacre was, in fact, a fortunate old man whose philosophical and humanitarian vocations had only declared themselves at the precise moment when Fortune—doubtless not as blind and far less spiteful than the vain multitude supposes—had finally heaped her favors upon him.

He was not scornful, as so many others are, of the infinitely honorable and lucrative business by means of which he had raised himself from almost nothing to a pinnacle of ten millions. On the contrary, he related with the naïve enthusiasm of an old soldier tales of countless battles fought against the competition, and delighted in remembering the sometime heroic gunfire of inventories.

He had simply abdicated, after the fashion of Charles Quint, the empire of fabrication, in order to embrace a superior life.

Having, in sum, the necessities of life, and being too old to be able to keep for much longer the keen eye of a businessman, and the arcane spontaneity that had disconcerted the situation and thwarted the schemes of competitors, he had had the wisdom to dispense advantageously of his commercial potency before the star of his health had begun to wane.

Henceforth, he would give himself, in an exclusive manner, to delights of the human sort.

Considering, with a touching lucidity, the nullity of plans thus far elaborated by cracked brains for the attenuation of poverty, and unshakably convinced, moreover, of the utility of the poor, he thought that there were better things to do than employ the financial and intellectual resources at his disposal to the relief of that rabble. In consequence, he resolved to apply the last glimmers of his genius to the consolation of millionaires.

"Who thinks," he said, "about the dolors of the rich? Perhaps only me and the divine Bourget, of whom my clientele are very fond. Because they accomplish their mission, which consists of amusing themselves in order to keep the wheels of commerce turning, one supposes too readily that they are happy, forgetting that they have hearts. People have the effrontery to contrast them with the coarse tribulations of indigents—whose duty, after all, is to suffer—as if rags and a lack of nourishment could be placed in the balance with the anguish of death. For such is the law. One can only truly die on the condition of possession. It is indispensable to have capital to render up one's soul, and that is what people cannot comprehend. Death is nothing but separation from Money. Those who have none have no life, and hence cannot die."

Full of such thoughts—more profound than he supposed—the whitener of sepulchers worked with all his might for the abolition of terrors. He had the honor of being one of the first to foment the generous conception of the Crematorium. The traditional horror of death, according to that thinker, was procured, above all, by the frightful image of decomposition. In the conferences of incinerators, who had elected him as their president, he recounted, unfurling them with all the eloquence of an orator, all the phases of hat subterranean chemistry. The thought of becoming for example, a flower, revolted his accountant's imagination.

"I don't want to be carrion!" he bellowed. "Immediately after my death, I demand to be burned, calcinated, reduced to ashes—for fire purifies everything. . . ."

Etc.

His wish was granted in full, as you shall see.

The excellent man had a son, as everyone who knows the value of money should.

I ask permission here to digress momentarily and to take flight in fulsomeness.

Dieudonné Labalbarie was, if I dare say it, even more admirable than his father. Conceived in a moment of signal triumph over temeritous competitors, he realized in full the ideal of the solid virtues on which the most serious houses of credit can count. At fifteen, he had already put aside savings, and his person was maintained like an account-book. Barrême[1] himself could not have discovered anything frivolous in him.

The height of injustice would have been to reproach him for a minute of enthusiasm, a spasm, even suppressed, of crazed affection for anyone or anything whatsoever. His happy father was obliged to support himself on his cash-box or his counter when he spoke, so intoxicated was he to have procreated such a boy.

That blessed child is alive and prospering. He has even doubled his patrimony in the three years that he has been an orphan, having been able to make himself adored by a wealthy turtle-keeper whom he has just married, and many people would doubtless recognize him, if I did not hesitate to offend the lily of his modesty by attempting to trace his pleasing image. Guess if you can; I shall not have said too much, perhaps, in declaring that he has the physiognomy of a handsome reptile, and that he is usually accompanied by a mastiff of monstrous dimensions.

---

1 The mathematician Bertrand-François Barrême (1640-1703), author of the pioneering textbook of accountancy, *Livre des comptes faits*.

Now, here is the infinitely little-known story of the death and funeral of his father. Connoisseurs of pleasant emotion are invited not to continue reading.

One morning, the official medical examiner established that the great Fiacre had ceased to exist.

Immediately, Labalbarie junior swung into action. Without wasting any vain tears, or wearing away the "fabric" of his own life—which is to say, time, according to the noble expression of Benjamin Franklin, which he quoted incessantly—he arranged and prepared everything without losing a second.

At ten thirty-five, the newspapers, having been informed of his mourning and the expression of his grief, scattered a thousand exemplars to all four winds—the announcements to be sent by mail had been judiciously ordered and printed some time in advance. Similarly for the black marble plaque destined for the Columbarium, which displayed a phoenix spreading its wings in the midst of flames and the terrifying inscription demanded by the deceased:

I SHALL BE REBORN

Dieudonné then went for a bicycle ride, in order to retemper the fibers by means of an energetic dose of air, dined copiously, received a few tearful visitors, went to make his devotions at the Bourse, carried out a few profitable recoveries in the evening and spent the night away from home in order to emphasize the extreme violence of his grief.

The next day, a sumptuous hearse decked with flowers and followed by a thinly distributed crowd took the remains of the deceased to the Crematorium.

Ha ha! You'll be reborn! the affable Dieudonné said to himself, left alone in the terrible furnace-room with the two men charged with his father's incineration. *We'll see about that!*

The bier, carefully fashioned in light planks, according to the regulations, in order to be rapidly devoured by an atmosphere of seven hundred degrees, rested on the mechanical cart whose two metal antennae, launched with force, plunge the dead into the furnace and came back, uttering a screech—a movement of diastole and systole that is executed in twenty-five seconds.

So, Dieudonné was there, doing his filial duty, when a sudden noise was heard inside the coffin.

Oh, a muffled and very vague noise, I assure you, but a noise all the same, like a false corpse trying to stir in its shroud. It even seemed that the coffin oscillated slightly. . . .

At the same moment, the door of the furnace, maneuvered with precision, opened wide.

The three faces, reddened by the atrocious flames, looked at one another.

"It's the body emptying itself," Dieudonné affirmed, tranquilly.

The other two hesitated, however.

"Get on with it, then, damn it!" howled the parricide. "I tell you that it's the body emptying itself." And he put a wad of banknotes into the nearest hand.

The antennae bounded forwards, and rebounded backwards.

The door closed, but doubtless not quickly enough, for Dieudonné, positioned directly opposite, thought he perceived, in the instantaneous blaze of the coffin, his father's two extended arms and despairing face.

The End of Don Juan

To Henry Cayssac[1]

It does one good to chat
with a man who has only one head.
Jules Vallès[2]

"AND the wretch died heaped with wealth, just as he had lived. He didn't even have the excuse of being a wastrel, a prodigal. He was, it's said, the best in the world at placing his capital advantageously. In the end, he died without any infirmity, in full possession of himself, although very old, like a patriarch before the deluge. That seems to me to be a bit much. Without demanding assiduously the finger of God, like a schoolboy raised by the good fathers, one would nevertheless have liked, for the

---

1 Henry Cayssac was another of Bloy's long-time correspondents and a close friend, in spite of his atheism. Cayssac's wife Henriette became notorious because of her liaison with the Symbolist writer Paul Leautaud. "Le fin de Don Juan" was originally published in the 10 novembre 1863 issue of *Gil Blas*.
2 The journalist Jules Vallès (1832-1885) was a diehard opponent of the Second Empire and a key member of the Commune; he managed to escape capture and thus avoided the execution to which he was sentenced *in absentia*.

sake of honor and justice, the death-throes of that male-factor to have been less gentle."

Thus spoke a man devoid of malice, clouding the insolent glory of the Marquis de la Tour de Pise.

The well-known individual in question had just expired. For a long time he had been thought to be eternal. Born in joyous England at the commencement of the emigration, when Louis XVI still had his head on his shoulders, popular rumor claimed that he was still virile in his nineties: an unverified prodigy, no doubt, but accredited by the enthusiasm of a few chill-fearing disciples who were past sixty themselves.

The fact is that Marquis Hector de la Tour de Pise emitted a radiance, like a monstrance. It was considered indisputable that queens had once been exhausted by love "on entering his bedroom," and that an entire population of Ariadnes was sobbing because of him. A long time before the celebrated Beauvivier, who consoles us, he had been able to submit his person to adjudications,[1] and even to share-issues. Hence his opulence. Until his final days, one saw the noblest families paying dearly for the dividends of his bed. . . .

Such, at least, was the legend universally accepted in regard to that heartbreaker, whose trouser-buttons, mounted in ear-rings, are presently regarded as inestimable jewels.

"My dear Monsieur," replied the Midwife, "You don't know what you're talking about. I wasn't present at the death-bed of that scoundrel, but I can assure you that no Ixion was ever more cruelly punished. Imagine everything you can, but you'll never attain that horror. So sit down

---

1 Properce Beauvivier is a character in *Le Désespéré*, a prolific novelist whose works include *L'Inceste*.

on that fetus which is holding out its arms to you and pay attention. I'm in a narrative mood his morning.

"Marquis Hector was a handsome man, that's certain, and he had all the appearances of a great lord—the envious have never been able to deny that. He was so different from the multitude that, as soon as he appeared, *everyone seemed to resemble him.*

"He could have had himself displayed in public for money, like a true monster. He contented himself with letting himself be seen in private for considerable sums, which he invested with extreme care in the most serious enterprises. Everyone knows the speculative flair he manifested in the midst of the worst complications—but that's of little interest. In an era when everyone is walking the streets, almost without exception, the prostitution of that gentleman and his financial aptitude are not surprising. The two things go so well together.

"I have much better to offer you, and it's a horror difficult to imagine that I promised you, isn't it? If your thirst for an expiation isn't appeased after my story, nothing is capable of appeasing it.

"To begin with, do you even know what there was to expiate? No. You imagine, like everyone else, the more or less odious life of a vampire exclusively occupied with his turpitudes for nearly a century, through which he ran like a gutter of putrefaction, having never looked into the faces of those in pain and suffering. A point of view as banal as a sermon, my worthy Monsieur. It was a case of something infinitely more delicate.

"You'll doubtless do me the honor of believing that I am unbound by professional secrecy, as any first-rate midwife ought to be—we leave that to the physicians who have no other means of avoiding prison most of the time.

"Well, I had the handsome Hector for a client. He was married twice and killed at least one of his wives, without having any need of my help in that task. He operated on his own, delightfully, and never had recourse to anyone. I had quite simply delivered his first, and then his second, ten years later, toward the end of Louis-Philippe's reign, just as I would have delivered porter's wives and prostitutes. The marquis had insisted on being alone with me on both occasions.

"The first time, we brought out a kind of goat-foot with neither eyes nor a mouth, which had, instead of a nose, a kind of flaccid membrane hanging down in a manner that I won't describe to you, impressionable man. La Tour de Pise, endowed with the self-composure of the dead, took possession of the abortion before I could stop him and offered it to the kisses of the mother, who died two hours later.

"The Marquis' second child had two heads on a spindle of a body, almost devoid of arms and legs, and there was another edition of the same image. This time, the mother couldn't see anything. I wrapped the little abomination in my apron and hurled myself out of the room. I lost the clientele of the noble lord by doing that, but I had divined many things, and I subsequently learned many more. . . ."

The terrible matron lowered her voice in a strange manner. "You're convinced now," she continued, "that I've just told you the Crime and the Punishment. That's already enough to relax the brass fiber of your implacable justice, as the catguts of a guitar on which fifty dogs have pissed relax. But you're still no closer than before, you hear?

"In our business one is at the very outlet of the sewer, and one sees such things come out that it eventually becomes difficult to be astonished. However, the man of which we're speaking has astonished me, and astonished me again, to the point of terror.

"If there had only been what you've just heard, that man would be no more, in the final analysis, than one more horrible rogue in the host of rogues, and would merit the punishment that has been mentioned, but I repeat to you that there's something else, and the punishment will make you tremble if you're capable of comprehending it.

"Have you noticed the bizarrerie of the similarity of the monstrous phenomena, reproduced at a ten year interval with two legitimate wives?—married for their money, of course; that goes without saying. I'm convinced that, had the experiment been repeated indefinitely, it would have produced the same result.

"To speak clearly, the marquis was an idolater—a fervent and rigorous idolater, internally configured in he resemblance of his God, but who could only reproduce it externally in his attempts at progeniture.

"He worshipped within himself, in a mysteriously-lit oratory, that part of his own body which the priests of Cybele once held in such great honor. He had had it molded on himself by a very skillful worker and the object, exposed in a sort of tabernacle, received every day the obsecrations of that Corybant, whom society believed to be a libertine—just as the small fry of the hospital interns have swallowed the conviction that the Buddhist Charcot is a physician. No one can ever know how many people are other than they appear in the eyes of their contemporaries.

"That, Monsieur, was his true crime: the supreme outrage for those who know and those who see into the depths. Everything else follows from that."

Now, this is the expiation that lasted ten years, until the eve of his death.

Every night, a very tall and exceedingly handsome old man, whom the proudest women had loved and who now knew all the streetwalkers, was invariably lurking in the shadows at the last hour of business. His tastes were known and the dialogue was engaged, as crapulous as possible on the part of the woman, utterly humble on his, for the insisted on playing the role of a dirty client consumed with inadmissible desires.

After a few minutes, measured by an infallible chronometer, an understanding was naturally reached.

The woman, leaning back on a wall, then offered him each of her feet alternately, and the octogenarian, wallowing on the ground—whatever the weather—licked the soles of her boots, moaning with ecstasy.

Such was the final demand of the little God of that vanquisher, whom three generations of imbeciles compared to Don Juan.

A Martyr

To Julien Leclercq[1]

"SO, Monsieur my son-in-law, it's really true that no religious consideration can act upon your soul. You can't even wait until tomorrow to commit your obscenities, I see all too clearly. You won't have any pity on that poor child, raised until today in the purity of the angels, and whom you're going to tarnish with your reptilian breath. Well, dear God, may Thy will be done and Thy holy name be blessed in all the centuries of centuries!"

"Amen," Georges replied, lighting a cigar. "Once again, my dear mother-in-law, be assured of my eternal gratitude. I'm relying entirely on your prayers, and believe me, I won't forget your exhortations. Good night."

The train moved off. Madame Durable, left on the platform, watched the express pull away, transporting the newly-weds southwards.

Still disturbed by the emotions of the day, but with eyes as dry as enamels fresh from the kiln, she tapped the sidewalk nervously with the tip of her umbrella.

---

1 Julien Leclercq (1865-1901) was a Symbolist poet and critic, a regular contributor to the *Mercure de France* prior to his premature death. "Une martyre" originally appeared in the 1 decembre 1893 issue of *Gil Blas*.

Angrily calculating immolations and sacrifices, she told herself, the dear soul, that it was truly very hard to have lived for twenty years purely for that ungrateful daughter, who was abandoning her thus, as soon as she was married, to go with a stranger manifestly devoid of decency, who would doubtless proceed, almost immediately, to profane her with his lewd touch.

"Oh yes, for sure, one has rewards, with children! Consider, then, Monsieur"—she was addressing herself almost unconsciously to the deputy station-master, who had approached her in order to exhort her politely to disappear—"that one brings them into the world with abominable pains, of which you can have no idea, one raises them in the fear of God, one tries to render them similar to angels in order that they might be worthy to sing indefinitely at the feet of the Lamb. One prays for them relentlessly night and day, for a third of one's life. One inflicts upon them, for the good of their tender souls, penances the mere thought of which makes one tremble. And this is the recompense! There it is! One is abandoned, dropped like a rag, like a piece of orange-peel, as soon as some guttersnipe of a man appears whom one has been stupid enough to receive in one's home because he appeared to be a good Christian, and who abuses the privilege immediately to soil an innocent heart to suggest impure visions, to make, if I dare say it, a young person raised in the most saintly ignorance believe the dirty caresses of a spouse of flesh will give her a more vivid joy than the chaste effusions of a mother's tenderness. . . .

"And you see what happens, Monsieur! You can bear witness to it on the Day of Judgment! I'm left, abandoned, betrayed, alone in the world, devoid of consolation and devoid of hope. Put yourself in my place."

"Madame," the employee replied, "I beg you to believe that I sympathize with your chagrin, but I have a duty to inform you that the demands of the service do not permit you to stand here any longer. I implore you, then, to my great regret, to be good enough to go away."

The dolorous mother thus dispatched, disappeared, not without taking heaven as her witness, one more time, of the immensity of her mourning.

Madame Virginie Durable, née Mucus, was the insufficiently admired type-specimen of the martyr. She was even a martyr of Lyon,[1] and, in consequence, the most atrocious shrew one could ever see.

Since her earliest childhood she had been delivered to the cruelest of executioners and had never known the refreshment of human consolation. The universe, moreover, was regularly informed of her torments.

Thirty years before, when Monsieur Durable, an oyster-merchant, now retired, had married that holocaust, the poor man had scarcely suspected the frightful responsibility of oppression that he was assuming. It did not take him long to find out, and to become, at length, entirely imbecilic in consequence. Whatever he might say or do, he had never once succeeded in not being criminal, in not trampling his wife's heart underfoot, in not driving thorns or blades into her.

---

1 The reference is to the martyrs of Lyon allegedly killed by the Romans after frightful tortures in 177 A.D., a report of whose fate, supposedly sent by the Church of Lyon to the Churches of Asia Minor, survived into modern times, although the authenticity of the document is dubious. The martyrs included St. Blandine, a seemingly frail young woman who allegedly wore out her torturers with her amazing fortitude.

Virginie was one of those amiable creatures who have "suffered a great deal," of whom no man is worthy, whom no one can understand or console, and who has not arms enough to raise to the heavens.

She displayed, it goes without saying, a sublime piety that it would have been ridiculous to claim to admire sufficiently and by which she herself was incessantly amazed.

In brief, she was an irreproachable spouse—oh, great God!—who must infallibly have attracted the rarest of benedictions upon the commercial enterprise of an evil-doing imbecile who did not understand his good fortune.

One day, a few years after the marriage, the martyr still being young and, it appeared, sufficiently tempting, the odious person had surprised her in the company of a scantily-dressed gentleman. The circumstances were such that he would have had to be not merely blind but as dead as a corpse to retain the slightest doubt.

The austere devotee who cuckolded him thus with an enthusiasm that was evidently shared, was not sufficiently literary to warrant the name of Ninon, but she was almost as handsome. She marched up to him, bosom in the wind, and in a very soft voice—a profoundly grave and gentle voice—she said to the stupefied man: "My friend, I'm in conference with Monsieur le Comte. Go about your business, will you? After which, she closed the door.

And that was the end. Two hours later, she signified to her husband that she no longer had anything to say to him, except in case of absolute urgency, declaring that she was weary of condescending to his shopkeeper's soul and complaining bitterly, in fact, of having sacrificed the hopes of a young virgin to a boor devoid of ideals who had the indelicacy to spy on her.

Being the daughter of a bailiff, she did not forget, on that occasion, to recall the superiority of her extraction.

From that day on, the Christian of the first centuries no longer marched without a palm, and existence became a hell, a lake of exceedingly profound bitterness, for the poor humiliated cuckold, who started drinking and became idiotic enough to be plausibly and charitably locked up in a lunatic asylum.

By virtue of a stroke of luck, Mademoiselle Durable's education had been better than circumstance might have led one to suppose. It is true that her virtuous mother, relentlessly applied to the brutalization of Monsieur Durable and indulging, in addition, in obscure farces, did not have much to do with it, having abandoned her at an early age to the mercenary vigilance of the nuns of the Escalier de Pilate, who, miraculously, carried out their mission conscientiously.

The young woman, sufficient endowed and eligible from every point of view, avidly seized the first opportunity for marriage that presented itself, as soon as she had seen through the ridiculousness and execrable malice of the old bitch, who then became a mother-in-law by a mysterious decree of redoubtable Providence.

The valor of the espouser was generally admired.

The ceremony was scarcely over when, the latter, very independently, declared his firm decision to depart immediately with his wife by express train. Everyone was able to see that the resolution in question, doubtless planned, did not disconcert the young bride in the least, who had appeared to pay only vague attention to the maternal moans and reproaches.

Madame Durable, beside herself with the most generous indignation, had therefore returned to her solitary house to meditate holy vengeance.

But no—the word "vengeance" is inappropriate. It was a matter for punishment. That outraged mother had the right to punish. She even had a duty to do it, in order that the fourth commandment of the divine law should retain its force.

Given that, any means became legitimate, pious intention being able to perfume the most venomous schemes.

In the execution of that praiseworthy design, the martyr was henceforth attentive to procure, by means of any intrigue or trickery, the dishonor of her son-in-law and her daughter alike.

The former was accused of monstrous vices, infamous habits certified by abominable witnesses. The young woman received letters that might have borne the postmark of Sodom.

Madame Culasse wrote to inform her of her grievances, and the brat Gros-Doigt let her know that "it could not be tolerated." A torrent of ordure submerged the conjugal bed of the newlyweds.

For his part, the husband was bombarded with an infinite number of anonymous or pseudonymous missives, various in form but always unctuous and saturated with the most affable sadness, informing him cautiously of the improper past of his wife, by the wind of which fifty young girls would be putrefied in the school dormitories, and who had certainly not been able to offer him, along with her dowry, the base and rudimentary virginity of her body.

The diabolical wickedness and infernal competence that moved the strings of that intrigue of imposture, which dosed the frightful poisons of infanticide on a daily basis, is indescribable.

That lasted for more than six months. The unfortunates, who had not wanted to feel anything at first but a profound scorn, were soon gripped by the horror of such a tenacious persecution.

They learned that letters from the same unknown source were scattered around them in the hotels, to the owners and servants alike, and to various notable individuals in the towns and villages through which they fled.

They were clawed by a continual anguished panic, raked by irreparable suspicions that they knew in vain to be absurd, finally falling into a sewer of melancholy.

They could no longer sleep, no longer eat, and their souls extravasated in the pale gulfs where hope dilutes.

Finally, one day, they died together at the same time and in the same place, without anyone being able to determine precisely in what manner they had ceased to suffer.

The mother, who followed them like a shark, had their suicide certified in order they could not have a Christian burial. She is evermore the Martyr, raising herself up every day to the Third Heaven, with extreme facility, and ringing the changes every evening, until late—according to the chronicle of the Rue de Constantinople—with a robust *valet de chambre*.

Suspicion

To Édouard d'Arbourg

THE number of imbeciles might be infinite, according to the canonical expression of Ecclesiastes,[1] but it would be difficult to encounter or imagine a more perfect idiot than the merchant of sphinx-oil whose much-publicized suicide has recently been reported, or could have been reported, in all the newspapers.

The history of celebrated cretins is cornered as soon as one has mentioned Aristobule. I ask permission to mask with that transparent anagram the patronymic of my hero.

Aristobule was born, to the astonishment of many, at the age of fifty-five—which is to say that, from the feeding-bottle onwards he manifested a prudence such that one would have supposed him three times the age of the majority of ordinary citizens. In his nappies, the amiable child was already suspicious of everything in the world. Taciturn by circumspection or only opening his mouth shrewdly, he drooled suspicion until the emergence of his dentition.

---

1 *Ecclesiastes* 1:15, rendered as "that which is wanting cannot be numbered" in the A.V., but as "the number of fools is infinite" in more modern versions.

His parents seemed themselves blessed by heaven to have engendered such a child, who, while not yet talking, was already keeping watch on the servants, having himself hoisted into chairs to verify the contents of cupboards and only consenting to go to sleep after having looked under all the beds.

A sly and dilatory schoolboy, he earned the abhorrence of his fellows by his sneak-like mannerisms and the hermetic silence in which the void of his evil heart was locked away.

The only thought that he seemed then, as afterwards and until the end of his miserable days, to be capable of excogitating, was that all people were, like him, concealing themselves with a continual, prodigious attention and that the most expansive and the most loquacious were precisely the ones of whom it was more necessary to beware.

When the dirty apple-trees of concupiscence began to flower within him, around his seventeenth spring, he did not oppose himself virtuously to the ram of temptation, but did his best to deceive it every time it pointed its horn, in order not to fall victim to the atrocious perfidy of women.

In sum, that flavorsome imbecile had, from the outset, something that gave the illusion of depth. He was a bastard of shadow, as Hugo puts it, a fetus of opacity, and he always gave the impression of floating in a jar of darkness.

One day, however, he got married. Business is indisputably business, and the prosperity of the commercial justification "Aristobule and Son" imperiously demanded that a suitable heiress enter into his bed, previously ignorant of promiscuities.

In all probability, no one will ever know what was accomplished in that mysterious bed, but a great number of details, collected with scrupulous exactitude, lead one to think that the molecules of the spouses must have come together slightly less often than the arrival of the precession of the equinoxes.

Conjugal fashion did not prevent Aristobule from being devoured by the jealousy of a young wild boar, the admirable effect of which was to enlighten his blockhead of a wife infinitely more effectively and rapidly than the most savant and suggestive affection could have done.

However ambitious I am to be unkind, I dare not contend that her lovers were as numerous as the stars, but I imagine that by grouping them in the middle of a vast plain one would obtain an appropriate contingent for the manifestation of an exalted patriotism.

The unfortunate manufacturer doubtless divined, or thought he had divined, many histories, but he was in the axis of such a furious whirlwind that he could never fix his rage upon a determined point—his wife's consolers could be compared to the invisible spokes of a cart-wheel passing by with inconceivably rapidity. It eventually drove him to doubt Arithmetic! Uncertainty and suspicion weighed so much upon that poor cuckold, whose intelligence darkened a little more every day, that he sank down to the inferior level where the atheists of Number crouch. Suddenly, he ceased to believe in the probity of figures. . . .

It was on that day of excessive tribulation, that hour of black distress and infinite dereliction, that a disinterested friend—perhaps the only one his wife had refused—came to warn him that a probable drop in the price of sphinxes would bring about his ruination if he did not take energetic measures immediately.

Aristobule, I think I have made it sufficiently clear, was suspicious of everything under the sun. In that regard, his intransigence was absolute. Suspicion was his vital principle, the tablets of his law, his supreme credo. He would have been a martyr to it. What am I saying? Had he not been one for forty years? In his commerce, surely one of the most considerable of our civilization, and perhaps of all those where reciprocal good faith is rigorously inviolate, the perpetual fear of swindles and snares had literally anguished, flagellated, clawed, tanned, trepanned, barbecued, twisted, quartered and harassed him every evening and every morning.

He had quarreled with a multitude of affable correspondents whose patience equaled that of a patriarch. He had missed out on regal deals that would have enriched him immeasurably.

In his company, full of disturbance and upsets, the agents succeeded one another in Indian file, without any of them being able to discover the platitude of genius that would permit him to immobilize his locomotive apparatus for twenty-four hours. It was, in sum, a miracle that failure had spared it.

One can therefore presume with what attitude the reckless friend was greeted who had, against all plausibility, been moved to pity for that animal, whose bankruptcy he foresaw. Immediately, Aristobule's resolution was fixed. He declared that his friend was a horrible scoundrel, a filthy traitor who was setting an infernal trap for him. In consequence, he did exactly the opposite of what he was advised to do, and, a few weeks later, was obliged to file for bankruptcy.

That ruination was a glimmer of light in his darkness. He thought, or thought he saw, clearly, that he had not been deceived. For the first time, he thought it fair that his wife should qualify him as a simpleton, a good-for-nothing and even a pimp, by virtue of a flagrant contradiction of terminology, for such was the first impulse of the wife in question.

However, he still dreaded being deluded.

"Why, then," he asked the prophet, giving the impression of some speaking from the depths of his cellar, "did you warn me?"

The other explained, simply, that he had feared poverty for him and his wife, even though Madame Aristobule had never deigned to take advantage of his consideration.

These veridical words—if it is permissible, with respect to such a subject, to borrow the respectable style of Holy Writ—renewed in the devastated soul of the businessman the youth of the meleagride, an animal described by Aristotle and believed to be the turkey.[1]

"The swine is talking about my wife!" he howled. "There must be something in it."

And immediately, he spoke rudely to her, accusing her brutally of having slept with the traitor.

But Madame Aristobule, who had a diabolical penetration of her husband's suspicious character, launched a reply at him that struck him as surely as a discus-thrower's discus.

"Yes, my dear, you're a cuckold."

---

1 In Greek myth the Meleagrides were the sisters of Meleager of Calydon, who were changed into birds (guinea-fowl rather than turkeys) to liberate them from the grief they felt after their brother's death.

That was, without any fear of contradiction, an affirmation, and in consequence, according to his theory, an imposture. The lie, then, appeared certain in every direction. He reset the black compass of his demented cretinism and, in despair of being *indubitably* a cuckold, killed himself.

Calypso's Telephone

To Marius[1]

MADAME PRESQUE could not console herself for the departure of Monsieur Vertige. In the six months since the pronouncement of their divorce had brought an equitable conclusion to their conjugal tribulations, that exquisite woman had gradually allowed herself to lapse into hypochondria.

The initial surges of a perfectly natural joy had rapidly been succeeded by the anxieties of solicitude, the alarms of insomnia, the grill of continence and, finally, bitter regret.

It was not that Monsieur Vertige was by any means an adorable man. Oh God, no! He stank like a ram, had a diabolical character and did not possess a globule of enthusiasm for his wife—but there was a piquancy about him, a mysterious quality that always makes women return to that kind of animal. It is doubtless inexplicable, but all too certain.

---

1 Possibly the Symbolist writer Marius Pouget, who employed the pseudonym Léo d'Orfer for his writings and editorship of the short-lived weekly *Le Capitan*, although the celebrated Anarchist Marius Tournadre is mentioned in Bloy's journals as an acquaintance, and might be the more likely candidate.

She was able to render herself the justice of having generously done, before their divorce, everything that a good wife can do in order to dislike her husband. She had even felt completely certain of success. She had had several lovers of an uncommon distinction. One could say unhesitatingly that the first, especially—oh, the first!—a senior employee in the administration of the Catacombs, who had, unfortunately, dropped her, was an ideal specimen.

Well, those fortunate endeavors and the favorable divorce that was their consequence had not been able to take full effect on her husband. She thought about the vile man continually and could not prevent herself from doing so.

Undoubtedly, she did not go so far as to deplore the fact that she was no longer Madame Vertige, but it became clearer to her every day that the banished spouse had been the indispensable condiment of her joys. In other words, love had lost its savor since she was no longer putting horns on a legitimate leaseholder.

It would be necessary to be the least of man not to know or to feel the extent to which divorce lifts hearts—but one is, at the same time, forced to recognize that it is not exactly a creditworthy institution, and Madame Presque was, as the familiar expression puts it, in a bind. Money had disappeared at the same time as Monsieur Vertige. It had disappeared as if into a gulf, and that circumstance had to count for something in the abandoned woman's present melancholy, as any thinking person can see.

Her amorous adventures had not been profitable—that was inevitable. In her truly puerile fear of appearing to prostitute herself, she had experienced the admirable ease with which gentlemen endure being freed of the importunate weight of paying restaurant bills, and the inconstant or ingrate individuals once feasted by her were not in any haste to come to her rescue. There was no bustle on the stairway of the tenth-rate furnished house that had replaced the comfortable apartment of old, and the question of everyday subsistence was becoming problematic.

At the height of that anxiety, a refreshing idea passed over her like a perfumed breeze over an arid spot. She had just remembered the telephonic apparatus that Monsieur Vertige possessed. The apparatus had often woken her up at night, and that was one of her innumerable grievances.

She had avenged herself for that by making use of that irresponsible vehicle of turpitudes and contemporary stupidities in various deceits. On fairly numerous occasions, Monsieur Vertige had been summoned to derisory meetings that forced him to absent himself for a few hours, of which his wife audaciously took advantage. At the office, he was believed to be overworked. The jokes had even gone so far as to cause anxiety that he might decide to stop responding.

Full of mysterious intention, Madame Presque therefore raced to the nearest booth and asked for a connection.

I shall open a parenthesis here, although it is completely unnecessary, to declare that the telephone is one of my pet hates. I claim that it is immoral to talk from so far away, and that the said instrument is an infernal device.

I cannot, of course, put forward any proof of the tenebrous origin of that *voice-extender*, and I am incapable of documenting my affirmation, but I appeal to the good faith and firm mind of people who have used it. Are not the ghostly noises that precede the conversation akin to a warning that one is about to penetrate into some reserved confine in which terror might perhaps be superabundant . . . if one only knew? And the horrible deformation of human sounds, which one might think drawn out by a roller-press, which only seem to have arrive at the ear after having been monstrously distended—is there not an element of panic in that too?

A few days ago, an old scientific bath-attendant, specifically appointed for the massage of useful discoveries at the hammam of an influential periodical, celebrated the glory of an English factory that is in the process of exterminating Writing. It appears that a luminous machine is about to destitute the human hand, which will no longer have any need to write—and the turncoat naturally invited people to rejoice at such progress. I imagine the telephone as a more serious crime, since it debases Speech itself.

"Hello? hello? To whom do I have the honor of speaking?"

"To me, Charlotte, your former wife."

"Oh! Very good. How are you, my dear Madame?"

"Not bad, thank you—and yourself?"

"Oh, personally, I'm getting a paunch. How can I oblige you, if you please?"

"Meet me as soon as possible, to discuss an urgent matter."

"Pardon me, Madame, but I have the honor of reminding you that we were not to see one another again."

"Well, my dear Ferdinand, my little Nand-nand, it's necessary to change that. What's the use of being divorced if we can no longer see one another?"

"What do you mean? Explain yourself, if you please," said the ex-spouse, the extremity of whose voice seemed to be dancing on the plate, on which Madame Presque planted a resounding kiss that the apparatus transmitted like a dart.

"Pay attention then, you big booby, and make an effort to understand me. When we were married, we acted like children and nearly made a mess of our entire lives, because we didn't understand anything—nothing at all—of what nature demanded of us.

"Free love, that's what we needed. Marriage is made for inferior beings and we had a higher calling. We would have been perfectly happy if we had been wise enough not to get married, not to live stupidly under the same roof, but to see one another amiably from time to time, like two piglets who adore one another.

"Why not realize that beautiful dream today? Do you think it's too late? Listen to me, you depraved man, and see whether I love you: *I will deceive everyone in the world with you*, my Ferdinand. . . ."

It is probable that Madame Presque knew in advance into what dung-heap of a soul that promise was to fall, for the two stumps of the serpent of adultery, severed by divorce and reconnected by the most sordid concubinage, were reintegrated.

Worn Out

To Henry de Groux

THE poor devil compared himself to the fox, to that other poor devil of a fox that he had come across one day, ten or fifteen years ago, in the middle of a wood.

It was the middle of winter. The limping animal, its flanks hollowed out by a long fast, almost incapable of continuing to drag itself along, had a thin hare dangling from its mouth, itself driven from its lair by famine, whose capture must have cost that father of foxcubs—doubtless awaited somewhere with a great deal of impatience— painful hours of lying in wait.

On perceiving the walker, the unfortunate vermin had tried to flee over the snow, but it seemed that it was completely exhausted, for it had been forced to stop almost immediately, without letting go of its prey—and the man, whose walking-stick was already raised, had suddenly lost the desire to strike such a wretched creature.

He had, therefore, quietly drawn away, satisfied with his clemency, but retaining forever the memory of the eyes of that suffering beast, which it had fixed upon him with an expression of the most intelligent despair.

That gaze, in which he thought he had discerned, at the same time as the rage of a beast at bay, something resembling human dolor, he had not forgotten; he had seen it again more than once, in moments of anguish, and now, that same gaze became more precise than ever, with cruel clarity.

"I took pity on that creature, though," he moaned. "Why shouldn't I obtain pity for myself?"

He too was awaited in his lair. Since he had left his sick wife and three children, so many hours ago, they had had time to die of cold and hunger—not to mention the amiable landlord, who must have profited from his absence to heap insults upon them.

What could he do? My God, what could he do? He had gone up and down a thousand steps. He had talked, requested, begged and wept, without obtaining anything. Dying of starvation, he could no longer walk, and began to envy that fox, which, at least, had something in its mouth. . . .

He had just left a very rich man whom he had believed to be exorable, having once rendered him one of those services that is not easy to forget. That neighbor, rutilant with ingratitude, had talked about his own disappointment in a gigantic enterprise in which he had missed out on a profit of several millions. He had politely escorted him to the stairway, nourishing him with the advice to seek manual work.

A few hours earlier, an individual of noble piety had deplored in front of him the abomination of hypocritical philanthropists and loquacious sociologists, and had ended up by awarding him a valuable recommendation to place his trust in God. That man of property, always ready to immolate himself, had not hesitated to sacrifice the delights of a conversation with numerous guests in order to

125

exhort the indigent brother, and in a private booth had ordered a single cup of excellent coffee, a good third of which he had given to his faithful dog.

And it was the same everywhere. Even the rain came out, in the end, against the despairing individual: a piercing black rain that soaked his heart. He thought then that he was in a kennel of demons, and at the same instant, judged worthy of collaborating in the salvation of the world.

Two paces away from him, an unknown man sheltering under the same coaching entrance was observing him attentively.

That unknown man, wanted by all the police forces in Europe, had one of those faces of putty, in which it seemed that the most complicated locks might be imprinted and on which a chiromancer might discover the lifeline of their bold picker: one of those modifiable and impersonal faces that do not appear to have any other employment than to reflect the pale fear of the multitude.

A sickly individual who could have been scythed down by a single punch unleashed by a feeble arm or ground down by no matter what heel without the most attentive pity being excited by it, without even the idea of any misfortune or prejudice awakening, so easy was it to divine the absence in him of any sublunary solidarity, he was one of those Beings engendered by silent Wrath, who have just enough human surface to incorporate the social Danger of which they are the frightful simulacra: strange parcels jolted about in express trains or transatlantic liners, to appear at the precise moment when the stalk of universal Anxiety sprouts in the hearts of the agonizing individuals that they outrage.

The resources of repression can do nothing about

them. They are as colorless and dilute as the dusk, and there is always a phantom that intervenes when the hand of the law reaches out to seize them.

But sudden Death obeys these defaulters, like a burglar's bitch, and Terror marches before them in velvet brodequins.

So the redoubtable unknown observed the man dying of hunger, and his unique eye, fringed with pale lashes, resembled a silver-tinted spider in the depths of it web.

"Funny, isn't it?" he said, all of a sudden. "A real joke to seek a crust among the bourgeois, when one's dying of hunger, when the kids are wailing and the sky's pissing all over you."

Hearing that faithful echo of his internal complaints, the vagabond could not help exhaling his lamentation.

"Oh, the swine. . . ." he sighed. Then, abruptly pulling himself together: "Do you know me then, Monsieur?"

"I don't know anyone," the other replied, "and the rabbit that can boast of knowing me is still in the drawer of a little mama who'll never whelp it. It's enough to look at you for moment, my poor chap. Your face looks like a doormat on which everyone in the world has wiped his boots. You haven't eaten for two days, I can see that by the way you pose your hind paws, and you have the glint in the corners of your eyes of a poor devil who isn't only suffering for his own carcass. Here, look at this advertisement. A hundred and twenty thousand hot from the mint for a squalid hovel with a garden and comfortable latrines. Quite a crust, eh? Well, you look to me like a notice for a sale by auction, and I can read easily enough that you could eat a roasted chicken. Come on, how much do you want for your skin? I'll buy it."

"Monsieur," the family man said in his turn, "it's wrong of you to make fun of me. I can assure you that I'm in no mood for jokes."

The stranger smiled in a way that made his ill-fitting black teeth seem even more livid.

"That's true," he said. "I'm joking. I sometimes put on farces that cause a certain resentment. I'm quite well known for it. But I don't always joke. Listen to me, and try not to make me repeat myself. I don't have a habit of chatting for as long as this. Here's a hundred-franc bill. Go fill up, stuff your family, burst them if you can, amuse yourself and come to find me tomorrow at Papa Bissextil's, 366 Rue Ramey. Ask for Monsieur Renard. That's agreed, isn't it? Good night."

It is necessary to believe that the generous fellow had a rare gift of penetration and knew exactly what he was doing, for the two men left the following evening for Barcelona, where they doubtless had important business to do.

A Failed Sacrilege

To Paul Jury[1]

O N the afternoon of that holy day, the peasant women
huddled here and there around the confessional suddenly drew apart with a most respectful urgency, in order
to make way for the Vicomtesse Brunissende des Égards,
who was coming toward the Tribunal of Penitence in her
finery.

The confessor was a simple fellow, a missionary of
the Congrégation des Lazaristes, sent to preach during
the Lenten fast in that rural area, still religious, and who
was giving the old curé a helping hand with the spring
cleaning.

The brilliant vicomtesse, who reigned over the entire
region and was, for the poor people of her fief, the arche-
type of magnificence, came rapidly and without hesitation
to kneel in the humble compartment dedicated to recon-
ciliatory confessions.

The missionary, having perceived her, hastened to ab-
solve a clog-maker's wife who was squeezed into the other

---

1 The psychoanalyst and theologian Paul Jury (1878-1953) is nowadays best-known for the posthumous publication *Journal d'un prêtre*
(1956; tr. as *Journal of a Psychoanalyst-Priest*).

booth, and almost immediately opened the porthole of exhortations to the considerable penitent that heaven had sent him.

The latter did not let him get a word in.

"Monsieur Preacher," she said, immediately, "I imagine that your time is precious and I'll begin by telling you that I only have a few minutes to spare myself. I'm impatiently awaited by my seventeenth lover, an adorable imbecile to whom I've resolved to deliver my body and soul in an hour or two.

"I'm an atheist, to the extent that one can be, and I do everything that it pleases me to do. I have a horror of poor people, I hate discomfort, and I'd rather have a bad conscience than a bad tooth, as a Jewish poet that you won't know put it so aptly.[1]

"I laugh at your blood-stained God and the absolution that you lavish on the good little folk of the village— but my husband is a virtuous député who has need of the admiration of his electors. What would people say in the locality if they learned that the Vicomtesse des Égards doesn't take communion at Easter?

"On the contrary, we have a duty to set an example, and I'm informing you that I shall have the pleasure of receiving the angelic bread from your hands at high mass next Sunday.

"Now, Father, I estimate that the normal time for an ordinary confession must have elapsed, the pious souls that surround us must be sufficiently edified as to my Christian sentiments, and it would be inexcusable for me to monopolize your ministry. I shall therefore retire modestly, as befits a sinner who has just been reconciled with her

---

1 Heinrich Heine (1797-1856).

Savior, praying that you will honor us as soon as possible with your presence at the château, where I shall strive very humbly to return your politeness at the holy table."

A minute later, the chatelaine, having prostrated herself at the altar, doubtless in order to say a fervent prayer, sailed out of the church like a frigate from a harbor, leaving behind a wake of strange perfumes, which the villagers respired like the rosemary of Paradise.

The next day, as soon as he had said mass, the preacher went up to Égards and had himself announced to Brunissende.

The right-thinking domestics admired in him an ecclesiastic of unusual lankiness, a kind of sacerdotal flamingo who might have been thought to be specially designed for seeking out lost ewes, or old silver drachmas that it is difficult to recover from under the furniture of rich dwellings in which disorder has settled in.

His strong face marked sixty years, as a step-ladder marks the great floods of a river, and his physiognomy offered, on this occasion, the spectacle of a ruminant generosity disturbed and harassed by an inexpressible nuisance.

He was introduced, but was obliged to wait for more than an hour, for everybody knows, nowadays, that the first duty of a priest is to wait for beautiful ladies to get out of bed, when they have the leisure or the condescension to receive him.

"Ah, my dear Father," said the Vicomtesse, who finally deigned to appear, "what a pleasant surprise! I precipitated myself out of bed in order to receive you, but I fear that I've kept you waiting—involuntarily, I assure you—and I'm counting on your charity to excuse a worldly woman who could not guess that you would be kind enough to wish her such a early bonjour."

"The sun rose five hours ago, Madame, and several million Christians are already suffering," the missionary replied, rather rudely. "Many of them are dying and despairing at this very moment. I would not have come to disturb you so early—nor even later, believe me—if the honor of God had not made it a pressing duty for me. I owe you a cruel night, Madame, and this morning, it seemed to me that a terrible angel dragged me by the hair all the way to your threshold. I am here to ask you whether you are prepared for death."

The lovely woman burst out laughing. "Death? That's admirable! Do I look as if I'm dying? Or do you take me for a criminal to be guillotined at dawn? And it's to tell me that that you got me out of bed at nine o'clock in the morning, like a street-sweeper? It's to make that frolicsome little speech that you disturbed yourself? Oh, come on, my dear Father, are you in your right mind?"

"I might ask you the same question, Madame," replied the priest, in a low voice that seemed to make some impression, "but I should doubtless do so in vain—I'm well aware of that. Have you forgotten already what passed between the two of us yesterday, in the church?"

"I know, Monsieur, that you received my confession at the sacrament of penitence, and that the secrecy of the confessional in inviolable. That's all I know."

There was a pause.

"It is up to me, then, to tell you what you don't know, or don't want to know. So be it. You have just issued an abominable challenge to God. Not content with hideously profaning, out of pure wickedness, the sacrament that you have the audacity to name, you have affirmed the intention of a more frightful sacrament. Naturally, you were counting on the silence of an unfortunate priest bound by his sacred character. I could perhaps reply to you that I do not have to keep the secret of a confession that does not exist, but these formulae are so holy that the pretence is equivalent to the act itself. I shall therefore keep silent.

"However, you are in danger, and I have a duty to warn you of that. There is still time. I implore you by the Blood of Christ that I consumed a little while ago, not to reduce me to becoming your judge."

"Oh, don't let that bother you, Monsieur Blood-Drinker—judge me as much as you like. That license granted, we're not exactly at the Revolutionary Tribunal, I implore you in my turn to put an end to this deplorable joke, of which I'm very weary, I can assure you."

"I shall withdraw, then," said the missionary. "This is my final word. Challenge for challenge. I don't know what God will do with your soul, and I tremble at the thought, but I sense that you will not be able, on Sunday, to accomplish the terrible action that you announced to me from the depths of your darkness. The glorious Christ is the bread of the poor, Madame, and it is eaten in the light."

Conclusion.

On Easter day the church was full, and Brunissende was on the bench, as the lady of the manor, more dazzling than ever.

The preacher was committed to celebrating that solemn mass. Having read the gospel of the Aromatics and the Resurrection, he stripped off his ornaments and appeared in the flesh.

He was extremely pale and resembled, in his surplice, the white-clad angel that the holy women saw at the Tomb.

Unexpectedly, he spoke on the text *Edent pauperes et saturabuntur*: the poor shall eat and be satisfied.[1]

He spoke for nearly an hour, as if he were waiting to run out of breath, as if he hoped to die by dint of talking, his speech becoming increasingly excited, until it became something frightful, luminous and supernatural.

That man devoid of eloquence was sublime. He expressed himself so well on the subject of poverty, that his ragged audience appeared as a congress of potentates, and in the end, the arrogant vicomtesse had the expression of a mendicant begging for her bread.

When the time came for the paschal communion, what happened was this:

When Brunissende was the first to kneel, the humble flock that was approaching suddenly drew back, as if before a wall of flames, and the priest, who was coming down the last step of the altar in order to advance, bearing the ciborium, toward the holy table, went back up precipitately.

They were obliged to purify the sanctuary, and every year, on the same day, a lavatory ceremony is scrupulously observed.

The Vicomtesse des Égards appears to be alive at present, but she is, in reality, more wretched than the inhabitants of graves. . . .

Thus was explained to me the political discomfiture of one of the most eminent puppets of the Moral Order.

---

1 The Latin formula in question was widely employed at the time as the standard grace pronounced before a meal. It is taken from Psalm 21.

"There's Trouble Brewing!"

To Edmond Picard[1]

THAT evening, there were about ten of us, the elect of eternity, at the home of Henry de Groux, the painter of murderers. We had been carefully selected in order that there should not be a single one of those people among us promised to the Academies, who could be satisfied with a derisory immortality.

It was firmly established in our councils that no one would ever admit either the beginning or the end of anything whatsoever, and would not descend to the abjection of imagining himself to be gratified by any kind of happiness.

We were the canons of Infinity, the protonotories of the Absolute, the medical executioners of every probable opinion and every respected commonplace. From time to time, I dare say, we were struck by lightning.

That evening, then, after ample and photogenic declarations on many subjects, it happened that a hunter of unicorns, as stubborn as he was subtle, renowned for his Hyrcanian doctrines and his hairless face, felt obliged to express himself in the following terms.

1 Edmond Picard (1836-1924) was a Belgian lawyer, politician and journalist

"Have you sufficiently noticed, my dear companions, the superior buffoonery of what is conventionally known as Repression? Persistent and jubilatory statistics inform us periodically as to the ebb and flow of transgressions of our penal laws. We enjoy synoptic catalogues in which are recorded—in Arabic numerals, naturally—the murders and thefts that help us to endure the monotony of the hours, and which the magistracy has punished without indolence, over such and such a period.

"There is, I assume, no need to contest the patriotic interest of these documents, at which conscientious philanthropists customarily raise their hackles and set their wattles aquiver. There is no more need, you will agree without blanching with rage, to undertake the divulgation of the universal crapulousness of honest people. Even the most notorious bandits and highwaymen would rise up against such a description of the moderators of social equilibrium.

"I believe, however, that I would be agreeable to you were I to offer the poem of a very banal experience that I had.

"Yesterday morning, going along the Rue Saint-Honoré, I perceived a venerable fellow coming down the steps of Saint-Roch. He was such a kindly old man that he spread a kind of warmth around him. On looking at him, one had the sensation of eating tender veal. His modest hands poured out all the clemency at his disposal, and his short stride gave the impression of a sugar mouse walking over the entrails of a rabbit. The heavens, which he was interrogating with one eye, were doubtless his friend, his most intimate comrade. He had undoubtedly been accomplishing exercises of piety with an indisputable fervor, and was surely on his way to fraternal practices that only the caresses of Heaven could reward, at a later date.

"I immediately concluded from that examination that a perfect eccentric was before me, and as I drew nearer I said to him, in a curt and low voice: 'Be careful, Monsieur, there's trouble brewing!'

"You know that it's not easy to astonish me. Well, my friends, the effect of those words disconcerted me to the extent of rendering me imbecilic for several hours.

"The individual went green about the gills, stared at me with the crazed eyes of a negro caught by a crocodile, started to quiver like an avenue of aspens, and hurled himself into a carriage, which immediately disappeared.

"That's what I had to tell you. I'm convinced that an analogous experiment, assuming that it is well-conducted, would give the same result nineteen times out of twenty. You only have to try it. Modern consciences are so indebted that it's within the power of any audacious individual to transform himself into a thunderbolt and to circulate like the Gorgon in the midst of honorable crowds."

"Of course!" cried the elephantine Rodolosse. "You've hit the nail on the head, my dear chap. I've been carrying on my person for several days a confidential letter that I'll read to you momentarily. I'm no ecclesiastic, bound to keep the secret of confessions, and besides, I'll stop short of the signature—but the confessions of its author confirm and certify to such an extent of joyous paradox what we've just heard that it would be impossible for me to deprive you of such conclusive testimony."

He exhibited a piece of paper. "This letter," he went on, "is from a well-known and perfectly honorable artist— do you hear me? Perfectly and absolutely ho-no-ra-ble.

"*Dear Monsieur, you did me the honor, a few days ago, of noticing a certain sadness on my part, which nothing dissipates and whose cause escaped you. You were persistent in trying to discover what it was. Today, I have decided to satisfy you.*

"*It is a terrible and passably dangerous secret that I have been carrying for fifteen years. You appear to have seen more profoundly into me than other men. Perhaps you will not be too astonished. Perhaps you might even feel some pity for a lamentable individual whom the world believes to be happy but is perpetually rent by atrocious remorse.*

"*At any rate, I shall surrender myself to you in the hope of being relieved of a part of that burden, more crushing every day. One ends up being forced to confess to someone, and I have chosen you in order not to be exposed to the temptation of addressing myself to the first gendarme I meet, since I do not have the courage to seek out a priest.*

"*Don't worry; it won't take long.*

"*In 187* I was twenty-five years old and I was dying of poverty. At that time, nothing enabled me to anticipate the future success and consequent prosperity that a few poor devils who have inherited my distress doubtless envy me today. I was then devoured myself by the basest and more hateful envy. Infatuated with the beauty of my soul and never doubting my genius, how could I tolerate vulgar people, definitive cretins and imperfectible cankers possessing homes, women, pigs and potatoes in impunity, while the greatest artist in the world slept under a roof of chaste stars?*

"*For I was homeless, without a penny in my*

pocket and sometimes even devoid of pockets—and
my adolescent stomach recriminated under the harsh
rule of the most insatiable appetite.

"Stimulated by a trafficker in human flesh, I
had undertaken the brokerage of insurance on the
lives of others but, not being able to sell the smallest
policy, I was literally dying of starvation in the coun-
try, striving to reach Paris on foot. . . ."

The reader paused. "At that point, Messieurs, the details and circumstances of location are given in such precise detail that I'm forced to omit a considerable number
of lines. You are, in any case, sufficiently edified as to my
correspondent's state of mind. I shall therefore skip to the
denouement.

"When I woke up, it was completely dark. It
was a delightful moonless night. It seemed to me that
I could cover the four or five leagues that still sepa-
rated me from Paris without any difficulty, but I was
so hungry that I was on the point of weeping.

"As I searched my rags mechanically for a piece
of bread, or a mouthful of anything at all, my hand
encountered an object that I took to be an old crust.
Immediately, I raised it to my mouth, roaring with
joy.

"It was a box of matches.

"I did not swallow it, that accursed box—that
infamous box whose presence I have never been able
to explain, and which had doubtless been sent to me
by demons. Something, however, descended within
me, something that seemed to me to be better than the

satisfaction of my intestines. I was saturated, drunk, refreshed by the delectable wine of hated and vengeance. I had noticed that a light breeze was blowing, in the direction of a small farm.

"Half an hour later, everything was ablaze. The inhospitable house became a mass of ashes, and I'm told that an old cripple died. The law never found the guilty party. . . ."

Our friend Rodolosse left it there, while a sculptor whose sickly beard I was contemplating swiftly turned off the lamp that was illuminating us, and I heard several people sobbing in the darkness.

The Silver Mote[1]

To Alcide Guérin,[2]
my favorite among my tales.

"HAVE pity on a poor clairvoyant, if you please!"
The most banal of stories. He had had the misfortune to be afflicted by clairvoyance in the wake of a terrible catastrophe in which a large number of honest men had died.

It was, I believe, a derailment on the railway, unless it was a shipwreck, a fire or an earthquake. It was impossible to find out for sure. He was reluctant to talk about it, and

---

1 The French title of this story, *Le Taie d'argent*, contains two double meanings, neither of which translates readily. The simple ambiguity of *argent* has been previously noted, but *taie* is more complex. Its medical meaning [leucoma] is obviously relevant to the central character's paradoxical condition, but Bloy's readers would have been far more familiar with its use in the standard French version of St. Matthew's account of the Sermon on the Mount, which, in the colorful English of the Authorized Version, calls attention to the kind of perspicacity that sees the "mote" in another's eye while overlooking the "beam," in one's own—a quotation that is crucially relevant to the subtext of the story.
2 Alcide Guérin published articles in a number of Symbolist periodicals as well as being on the editorial staff of *Gil Blas*, whose editor was his brother.

whether out of caution or subtlety, always hid it from the insulting curiosity of charitable individuals.

I still remember his decorative supplicant presence under the basilicary porch of Saint-Isidore-le-Laboureur, where he asked for alms, for his ruination was absolute.

It is impossible to resist the respectful compassion provoked by such rare misfortune so nobly supported. One sensed that the individual in question had once known, doubtless better than many others, the precious joys of blindness. A brilliant education must certainly have refined in him the estimable faculty of seeing nothing that is the privilege of all humans, almost without exception, and the decisive criterion of their superiority over simple brutes.

Before his accident he might have been, one divined sympathetically, one of those remarkable blind men called to be the ornament of their fatherland, and there remained to him from that epoch the melancholy of a prince of darkness exiled to the light.

Offerings, however, did not rain down into the old hat that he always held out to passers-by. A mendicant struck by such an extraordinary infirmity disconcerted the munificence of devotees of either sex, who made haste, on perceiving him to penetrate into the sanctuary.

Instinctively, people were suspicious of a needy person who could see the sun at noon. That could only be explained by some exceptional crime, some unspeakable sacrilege whose fatality he was expiating, and parents pointed him out to their offspring from a distance as a living testimony to the redoubtable sentences of God.

There was even a momentary fear of contagion, and the curé of the parish had been on the point of expelling him. Fortunately, a group of honorable scholars, whose competence cannot be put in doubt, had declared, not without bitterness but in the most peremptory fashion that "that would not do."

He lived meanly, therefore, on rare alms and the meager fruits of futile labors in which he excelled. He had no peer for threading needles. He even threaded pearls with a surprising rapidity.

Personally, I was forced, at one time, on several occasions, to have recourse to him in order to decipher the works of a renowned psychologist who had adopted the habit of writing with quadruply-divided camel-hairs. That was how we became acquainted and formed the regrettable intimacy that was one day to cost me so dear.

God forbid that I should be hard on a poor monster who, fortunately, has been dead and buried for a long time, but you can imagine how deadly the influence on my young imagination must have been of a individual who taught me the secret magic—forgotten for so many centuries—of distinguishing a lion from a pig and the Himalayas from a heap of bran.

That dangerous knowledge nearly doomed me. It would not have taken much for me to share the destiny of my teacher. I had almost got to the point of no longer being able to *grope*. That word says it all.

My lucky star, thank heaven, saved me from that gulf. I was able to disengage myself gradually from that baneful ascendancy, break the spell definitively and put on a good face once again among the moles and *quinze-vingts*[1] who nowadays enjoy the blind-man's-buff of life. But that took

---

1 *Les Quinze-Vingts* [literally, the Fifteen-Twenties] was the name of a famous hospital for the blind in Paris, whose name was adopted as a common noun for application to blind people.

time—a long time—and I was reduced to spending a considerable fraction of my income on the famous dexterity of an oculist from Chicago, who removed me definitely from the light.

I wanted to know, however, what had become of the terrible mendicant, and this is exactly how he ended.

For another few years he continued his mendicity as a clairvoyant at the door of the cathedral. His malady, it is said, got worse with age. The older he got, the more clear-sighted he became. The alms diminished proportionately.

The curates still gave him a few copper coins to salve their conscience. Unsuspecting strangers or people belonging to the lowest classes, and who very probably had the secret principle of clairvoyance within them, sometimes helped him. The blind man at the other door, a just and compassionate man who enjoyed good takings, gratified him with a humble offering on days when the bells rang incessantly. But all of that was really very little, and the repulsion he inspired, augmenting every day, gave him reason to think that he would not take long to die of starvation.

One could believe that he had sworn an oath to do that. Cynically, he displayed his infirmity, as the legless, the goitrous, the ulcerous, the one-armed and the rachitic displayed theirs, at votive feasts and in the country. He put it under your nose, forcing you, so to speak, to breathe it in.

Public disgust and indignation were at their peak, and the beggar's situation was only hanging by a thread, when something happened that was as prodigious as it was unexpected.

The clairvoyant came into an inheritance from a great-nephew in America, who had become insolently rich in the falsification of guano and had been devoured by the cannibals of Araucania.

The ex-mendicant did not claim his remains, but realized the succession and went on the spree.

One might have thought that the implausible and quasi-monstrous lucidity that had made him famous would immediately have gone into overdrive, like the "galloping" phthisis that is precipitated by profligacy. It was exactly the opposite that occurred.

A few months later, he was completely cured, without any surgery. He lost all clairvoyance and even became completely deaf.

No longer living for anything but rinsing his gut, he was finally liberated from the external world by *a silver mote*.

A Well-Nourished Man

To Eugène Grasset[1]

*M*ONSIEUR, *I regret to inform you that Monsieur Vénard Prosper of 13 Salle Souley, died at ten o'clock in the morning on the seventeenth of October 1893. I beg you to make known immediately your intentions relative to the disposal of the body, which must be removed within twenty-four hours, and, at the same time, to bring the necessary documentation—birth- or marriage-certificate—permitting the death-certificate to be properly drafted.*

It was by means of that note, bearing the address of the Hôpital Necker, that I learned last month of the inglorious death of one of the best-nourished men ever observed beneath the mountains of the moon, since the great Touranian gluttons whose epics have been transmitted to us by Rabelais.

I am honored to have been his friend and proud of

---

1 The Swiss artist Eugène Grasset (1845-1917) was a pioneer of Art Nouveau, who taught in various Parisian art schools from 1890 onwards.

146

having shared a few of his feasts, but I do not know how it came about that I remained alone among a multitude when the inexplicable emaciation arrived that was to consume him at the age of thirty-five. The unfortunate fellow had no one but me to visit him in his last days and to arrange his funeral.

I did my best, glad to spare the cadaver the odious profanations of the amphitheater and the terrifying final humiliation of the crematorium in which the Assistance Publique, ever maternal, has indigents who die in their dens burned without their permission. For the poor do not even own their carcasses, and when they lie in the hospitals after their despairing souls have fled, their pitiful and precious bodies, promised to eternal resurrection, O dolorous Christ, they are taken away with neither cross nor orison, far from your churches and your altars, far from those beautiful consoling stained-glass windows where your friends are depicted, to serve, like the carrion of filthy animals, for the experimentation of pork-butchers or makers of dust. . . .

Forgive me, though; I was about to lose sight of the fact that this is a story saturated with consolation, and which the most disillusioned optimists will, I hope, not be able to read without a certain tender sensation.

My friend Vénard practiced, with a kind of genius, the most neglected of the arts. He was not merely an illuminator, he was the renovator of Illumination and one of the most incontestable of contemporary artists.

He told me that, although he had made quite extensive studies in drawing in his youth, that singular vocation had been revealed to him later, when he returned from a famous expedition in which he had almost perished and, his patrimony having disappeared, poverty constrained him to find some means of earning a living.

In every epoch, that man of action, chained to the grill of his faculties, had tried mechanically to deceive them by the application of his hand to the miscellaneous ornamentations with which he overloaded, in his hours of heavy leisure, the surprisingly laconic letters that he wrote to his friends or his mistresses. One could exhibit three-word messages from him arranging meetings, in which amorous amplification was replaced by a brushwood of arabesques, impossible foliage, in extricable spirals, monstrous exotically-colored faces, in which the few syllables politely expressing his pleasure imposed themselves rudely on the eye in Carlovingian uncials or Anglo-Saxon characters—the two most energetic forms of inscription since the rectilinear capitals of the consular ephemerides.

A Gothic scorn for all underhand practices had given him a need, and a passionate taste for those venerable forms, into which he entered his thought as he might have put his limbs into a suit of armor.

Gradually, the ornamented letter had inspired in him the ambition of the historiated heading, and then the miniature detached from the text, with all its consequences, in conformity with the progress of that primordial art and generator of other arts, commencing with the poor transcription of Merovingian monks to end up, after half a dozen centuries with Van Eyck, Cimabué and Orcagna, who continued on canvas, with more material colors than the Renaissance was to abuse, the esthetic traditions of the spiritual Middle Ages.

His skill became prodigious as soon as he had decided to exploit it, and a marvelous artist appeared, of the most unexpected originality.

He had studied with care and incessantly consulted the adorable monuments conserved in the Bibliothèque Nationale or the Archives, such as the Gospel-books of Charlemagne, Charles the Bald and Lothaire, the Psalter of Saint Louis, the Sacrament-book of Drogon of Metz, the celebrated Books of Hours of René d'Anjou and Anne de Bretagne, and the sublime miniatures of Jehan Fouquet, Louis XI's official painter.

He had used every base stratagem to obtain authorization to copy a few Biblical scenes or landscapes from the magnificent Hours of Charles V, owned by the Duc d'Aumale.

Finally, one day, he had undertaken a costly pilgrimage to Venice, purely to study the miraculous Breviary of Grimani, in which Memling was said to have had a hand, and which had inspired Dürer.

Nevertheless he never reproduced, except in juxtaposed fragments, the work of his Medieval predecessors. His compositions, always strange and unexpected, whether they were Flemish, Irish, Byzantine or even Slavic, were really his, and had no other style than his own—the Vénard style, as Barbey d'Aurevilly said, precisely, in a newspaper article full of enthusiasm, which launched the illuminator's reputation.

Disdainful of the chloroses of water-color, his unique method consisted of painting in gouache, with full impasto, exasperating the violence of his color reliefs by the application of a particular varnish of which he was the inventor and which he did not surrender to anyone's analysis.

His illuminations, in consequence, had the gleam and luminous consistency of enamels. There was a feast for the eyes, at the same time as a powerful ferment of reverie for imaginations capable of making the rump of the Chimera recoil and reintegrating defunct centuries.

It now remains for me to explain why that extraordinary individual was such a well-nourished man, and how his lamentable end can be, for many people, an occasion for consolation.

It is well-known that I never miss an opportunity to promote the value of my contemporaries, and that it is a need for me to spread over suffering hearts the balm of my adjectives. Here, fortunately, I have almost nothing to do. I even wonder whether moral grandeur has ever been so glaring as in the occurrence of the illuminator's decease.

Prosper Vénard was not yet buried when, already, twenty articles penned by just writers had mentioned and complained about the unknown causes of his fall.

The illuminator had thought of nothing but eating. For ten years no one had seen him occupied, so to speak, in anything but the quest for nourishment. It would have been necessary to open the public treasuries to obtain his satiation, and all the flocks of Mesopotamia would not have satisfied the voracity of the deceased in question.

But finally, thank God, it came to an end. The cyclone of that hunger had dissipated. Other humans, in their turn, were allowed to work their lower jaws, and French society, delivered from a great peril, was once again able to sit down tranquilly at table.

Revelations flowed. "I nourished him for two years," said one. "He came to dine with me incessantly," cried another. "I never saw him once without him complaining of dying of hunger," said a third.

It was discovered, with amazement, that Vénard had been stuffed by everyone, without exception. More than five hundred people, perhaps, had been exclusively occupied from morning to evening in filling him up, and if he had died of languor, as the chief administrator at the hospital so strangely affirmed, it was because he had never had anything to do there and would have been wiser to renounce it, etc.

"Let's not mince words," wrote one of our most adipose critics. "It's disappointing, and it's profoundly inequitable. One has a right, at least, to the fat of pigs that feed at such great expense. That gentleman was not even capable of the most vulgar gratitude."

That was, in fact, true. My friend the thin Vénard ate quite well, I don't deny it, when he had the opportunity—which happened, I believe, a little less often that the conjunction of Neptune and Jupiter—but he did not lick his lips. No one could ever make him understand that a poor artist has a duty to suck the rind of a literary abortion that will regale him with peelings one day, and that the greater an artist he is, the more he has that duty.

He had even less understanding of the principle that the loan of a hundred-sou piece ought to engage him eternally in the toils of gratitude and that he was disrespectful to the important people whom he disliked—hence his reputation for ingratitude.

I have tried hard to defend him. I have even pushed audacity so far as to say that it might be the case, after all, that a few meals devoid of sumptuousness were redeemed a million times over by works of illumination of an incomparable magnificence, about which no one breathed a word, and which the exile of the Middle Ages had simply offered to his benefactors.

But my mouth was shut by making the observation to me that the unsalable polychromies of that eater will only have an interest of sorts for men of the second half of the twentieth century, an epoch designated by a few prophets for the resurrection of Barbarossa or Charlemagne.

In the meantime, the legend is indestructible, and the Ducs or Margraves emerging from the entrails of Anarchy who will govern Europe in a hundred years will perhaps give territories in exchange for a few miniatures by that Vénard, so famous once for his gluttony, and whose unfortunate contemporaries wore themselves out in feeding him well.

The Bean

To Alphonse Soirat[1]

A handsome young man and a
beautiful young woman got married
enthusiastically. After the ceremony,
alone at last, sitting facing one another
on comfortable chairs, they looked at
one another for a long time without
saying anything, and died of horror.
　　(A précis of contemporary history.)

MONSIEUR TERTULLIEN had just passed fifty, his hair was still beautifully black, his business was going admirably and his consideration was growing every day, when he had the misfortune to lose his wife.

It was a terrible blow. It would have required perversity to imagine a more satisfactory companion. She was twenty years younger than her husband, had the most pleasing face that one could ever see, and a character so delightful that she never let an opportunity to delight escape.

---

1 Alphonse Soirat was the publisher of Bloy's novel *Le Désespéré*. He also published the short-lived periodical *Le Symboliste* (1886), edited by Jean Moréas and Gustave Kahn.

The magnanimous Tertullien had married her without a sou, as do most businessmen inconvenienced by celibacy and who do not have the time to apply themselves to the seduction of difficult virgins.

He had married her "between two cheeses," as he said, merrily—for he was a wholesale cheese-merchant and he had accomplished that serious feat in the interval between a memorable delivery of Cheshire and an exceptional arrival of Parmesan.

That union, I am sorry to say, had not been fecund, and that was a shadow on the gracious scene.

Whose fault was that? A serious question that still weighed upon the fruiterers and grocers of the Gros-Caillou. A bristly butcher that the handsome Tertullien had disdained had accused him openly of impotence, to the scornful objections of a granulose mattress-maker, who claimed to have evidence to the contrary.

The pharmacist, nevertheless, declared that it was necessary to wait before forming an opinion, and the benevolent mass of disinterested concierges of litigation approved of that thinker's circumspection. The latter argued that Paris was not built in a day, that all's well that ends well, that he who has far to travel is careful of his mount, etc., and that, in consequence, there was reason to presuppose the favorable event that would, one day or another, put the final touch to the cheese-dealer's dazzling prosperity.

One might have thought that it was a matter of a Dauphin of France.

There was great emotion when the news spread of the sudden death that cut down such legitimate hopes.

Unless Tertullien remarried promptly—a hypothesis of which his grief did not permit the acceptance for a single minute—the future of his establishment was fried, and that child of his own labor, already so rich although started from nothing, would ultimately see its clientele pass to a foreign successor: a dark prospect that would embitter the regrets of the mourning spouse considerably.

The latter seemed, in fact, to be on the point of falling into a gulf of despair.

I do not know to what extent the dream of a cheese-dealing dynasty worried him, but I was the auricular witness to his dolorous bellowing and the extra-judiciary summonses that he issued to himself to follow his Clémentine to the grave within a short period of time—which, however, he did not fix.

Having had the leisure to study that likeable man in depth, by virtue of maintaining the closest of commercial relationships with him for ten years, I had been able to observe an admirable, though little known, trait of his character. He had an atrocious fear of being cuckolded. All his ancestors had been, for two or three hundred years, and his affection for his wife was based, above all, on the unshakable certainty of being completely assured of her integrity in that regard. His gratitude even had something profoundly ludicrous and poignant about it.

On reflection, that ended up by becoming a little tragic, and I sometimes wondered, with amazement, whether Clémentine's scandalous sterility was explicable by any other means than certain strange doubts that Tertullien might have about his own identity, and by a sublime dread of cuckolding himself by fecundating her.

But all that was too fine, too far above Marolles, Bondons and Livarots,[1] and the banal event that had infallibly to arrive, arrived.

---

1 Regional varieties of cheese.

Clémentine having made restitution of her soul to the Lord, the unfortunate widower initially exhaled, impetuously, the moans and sobs that nature recommends. When he had paid that first tribute—to make use of an expression of which he was fond—he wanted, prior to the funeral ceremony whose certain stress caused him to shrink in advance, to put the adored one's relics in order personally.

That was where his unkind destiny was lying in wait for him. The derisory labarum[1] of the Tertulliens appeared to him.

In a mysterious drawer of an intimate item of furniture that the most distrustful of husbands would never have taken it into his head to suspect, he discovered correspondence, as voluminous as it was varied, that did not permit him to cling on to illusion for a second.

All his friends and acquaintances had passed that way. With the sole exception of myself, all of them had cherished his wife. Even his employees—he found letters from employees on pink paper—had been simultaneously gratified.

He acquired the certainty that the deceased had deceived him night and day, whatever the weather, almost everywhere: in his bed, in his cellar, in his grain-loft and even in his shop, under the eyes of the Gruyere and in the effluvia of the Roquefort and the Camembert.

Needless to say, that indecent correspondence did not spare him. He was relentlessly mocked from the first line to the last. One telegraph office employee renowned for

1 The labarum was the standard on which the Roman emperor Constantine, after his victory over Maxence, had a cross and the monogram of Jesus Christ inscribed.

his wit joked, in a manner as unkind as possible, about his commerce, to the extent of allowing himself allusions or counsels that it is impossible to publish.

But there was one extraordinary, exorbitant, fabulous thing to unbalance the constellation of Capricorn. Appended to that mortifying dossier was an interminable series of little sticks, which astonished him and whose presence seemed inexplicable at first. Summoning up the sagacity of a subtle Apache on the war-path, however, a sudden enlightenment inundated him when he perceived that the number of these objects was exactly the number of adorers encouraged by his unfaithful wife, and that each of them bore a number of notches cut with a pen-knife, like those inflicted on butchers' chopping-boards. Evidently, Clémentine was a very orderly woman who kept strict accounts.

The husband, crushed by humiliation, expressed the very natural desire to be left alone with the dead woman, and shut himself in for two or three hours, like a man who wants to deliver himself without restraint to his affliction.

A few weeks later, Tertullien hosted a sumptuous dinner on the day of Epiphany. Twenty male guests, selected with care, crowded around his table. An unparalleled magnificence was deployed: exquisite, abundant and unexpected fare. It resembled the farewell feast of an opulent prince on the point of abdication.

Several guests, however, experienced a moment of anxiety at the sight of the funereal décor that the henceforth-lugubrious imagination of the cheese-merchant had doubtless borrowed from some remembered melodrama. The walls, and even the ceiling, were hung in black; the tablecloth was black; the illumination was provided by black candelabra in which black candles were burning. Everything was black.

The telegraph office employee, completely taken aback, wanted to leave. A jovial pig-breeder held him back, declaring that it was necessary to "rise above it" and that he thought it "very funny."

The others, momentarily hesitant, decided to snap their fingers at death. Soon, the bottles were circulating without interruption, and the meal became utterly hilarious. By the champagne, the success of the décor was assured and lewd jokes were putting in an appearance, when a gigantic gateau was brought in.

"Messieurs," said Tertullien, rising to his feet, "we shall raise our glasses, if you please, to the memory of the dear departed. All of you knew her, and appreciated her heart. You cannot have forgotten her amiable and tender heart, can you? I pray you to penetrate yourselves, in a very particular fashion, with her memory, before this epiphany cake is cut, which she would have loved so much to share with you.

Having never been the lover of the cheese-merchant's wife, probably because I had never met her, I had not been invited to that dinner and do not know who got the bean.[1] But I do know that the diabolical Tertullien was disturbed by the law for having inserted into the enormous loins of that frangipani the heart of his wife: the putrefying little heart of the delightful Clémentine.

---

1 The reference is to a custom akin to the English practice of baking a small coin into a Christmas pudding. In France and many other Catholic countries a trinket of some kind is baked into a "king cake" celebrating the arrival of the Magi at the Epiphany. In earlier eras a bean had been baked into the cake, and the person who got the bean became the "king" of the feast.

Digestive Proposals

To André Noell[1]

ALL stomachs being full, it was decided to put an end to the poor.

At ten o'clock in the evening, about thirty sublime plantigrades had fallen into agreement on the issue that fraternal "nonsense" had gone on for too many centuries, and that it was expedient to pour an ample reprobation over the ragged class that takes a malicious delight in breaking the hearts of well-dressed folk.

Various motions were expectorated.

The Psychologist cooed that there is nothing as beautiful as pity—the true judicious pity that is excited by the groans of the rich—and that it is a social crime to encourage the idleness of beggars. He added that an enlightened administration would be concerned, above all, to protect against the latter the distinguished intelligences and "delicate souls" who conserve the traditions of aristocratic elegance and sensibility.

The conclusion was belched by Francisque Lepiou, a

---

1 Presumably the André Noell who published "La Chanson des mousquetaires" in *L'Illustre du Soleil du Dimanche* in 1893, about whom further information is hard to come by.

159

fat philosopher full of energy, who demanded frankly that every French citizen incapable of justifying an annual income of three thousand francs should be sent to the most insalubrious penal colonies.

A free man who had had misfortunes in Constantinpole, and had made himself famous by singing like a nightingale in the Sistine Chapel about universal suffrage, supported that judicious avowal with flute-like chirping.

Several mucilaginous and inextricable poets enumerated the afflictive punishments that a vigorous repression ought to exercise against the impenitents or recidivists of poverty. Fusillades, blasts of grapeshot, drownings, auto-da-fés, banishments and mass deportations attracted successive cries of enthusiasm.

It even transpired that a bibliophile, having a rare first edition on his person of the famous *Bottin des Supplices*, printed in fourteen languages at the beginning of the nineteenth century at King-Tcheou-Fou on the borders of Kiang by the Plantin of the Celestial Empire, read a few pages and made the entire audience weep with compassion.

I would never finish if I undertook to report the transcendent apophthegms recited on that occasion by the bejeweled women who were there, and whose reasoning, as everyone knows, is so superior to that of men. Besides which, will all that not be taken as read when you know that all this happened in the home of the dazzling Vidamesse du Fondement, whose exceedingly happy spouse has covered himself with glory by negotiating the bilateral treaty—so long considered in European cabinets as an unrealizable dream—that will henceforth unite, finally, the Principality of Sodom with the French Republic?

My historian's conscience will not permit me to omit a bizarre and passably indecipherable individual whose precarious attire was astonishing in such a milieu. He was familiarly nicknamed Apemantus and he was the Cynic.[1] That precious quality won him a kind of welcome in certain ultra-superfine groups that aspired to the supreme Athenianism.

"On what do you live?" he was asked, wickedly, one day, in the presence of fifty people, by the most peevish of poetesses.

"On alms, Madame," he replied, simply, with the coolness of a dead fish—a response that, although inexact, characterized him very well.

People did not irritate him too much, knowing that he had a cruel bite, and he sometimes unsheathed a sort of barbaric eloquence that captured the attention of the most stubbornly inattentive and cringingly delicate individuals. In sum, he said whatever he wished—a rare privilege that no one contested.

The mistress of the house asked him, therefore, on that evening, to express his sentiment.

"It will, alas, require a story," Apemantus said, "a story as unkind as possible, it goes without saying. But first, you will submit—without understanding any of it, I'd like to believe—to a few reflections or preliminary conjectures that I need to make in order to stimulate the narrator in me.

"It is unfortunately indisputable that poverty contaminates the brilliant face of the world, and it's utterly

---

1 Apemantus is a cynical philosopher featured in Shakespeare's *Timon of Athens*, who exchanges witty insults with Timon before and after his fall from grace.

untoward that ladies full of perfumes should so often be exposed to encountering little children dying of hunger.

"I know full well that there is the resource of not seeing them, but one senses, all the same, that they exist; one hears their inharmonious supplications; one even risks catching a little vermin—you are familiar, ladies, with that ignoble pedicular vermin that 'does not allow itself to be caressed as easily as the elephant,' as our great poet Maldoror put it, and which gladly abandons the needy in order to burrow into inestimably costly muffs or stoles.

"All that plunges me into a very bitter affliction, and I applaud delightedly the noble idea of a general immolation of indigents. Nevertheless, while awaiting the good news of massacres, would it be permissible for me to ask those among you who have never scratched, whether they have ever been able to observe, without a telescope, the unequal division of philosophical certainty with regard to a few pretended axioms?

"To put it another way, where can a man be found, not yet verified and catalogued as a born idiot or an imbecile, who would dare to say that he has not a shadow of doubt about his own identity? For that is the point.

"Quite ingenuously, I declare that sometimes, when thinking of the story in the gospel and the astonishing number of swine necessary to provide comfortable lodgings for the impure demons emerging from a single man, it has occurred to me to look around fearfully. . . ."

"Pardon me, Monsieur," said a paleographer, "but it seems to me that you're going a bit far."

"I'm on the right track, then," the imperturbable fellow replied, bowing, "for far is exactly where I want to go." He continued: "Look, I'll condescend to be entirely clear. What is, in our most accredited literature—I mean newspaper serials and the theater—the supreme, irresistible, indefectible, primordial and fundamental trick? What is, if I might put it thus, the string that breaks everything, the certain arcanum, the *Open Sesame* that opens caverns of pathetic emotion, infallibly and divinely exciting crowds?

"My God! It's very silly, what I'm about to tell you. That famous secret is, quite simply, uncertainty regarding the identity of individuals. There is always someone who is not, or might not be, the person one supposes. It's necessary that there should always be a son that one does not suspect, a mother whom no one has foreseen, or a more-or-less sublime uncle who is in need of being disentangled from the chaos. Everyone ends up by recognizing the person in question, and it is a source of tears. That hasn't changed since Sophocles.

"Don't you think, as I do, that that imperishable power of a banal idea is founded on some symbol, some very profound presentiment, sought for three thousand years by the inventors of fables, like a blind and desperate Oedipus searching for the hand of his Antigone?

"We were talking about the poor, weren't we? Here we are, then. That emotional device is inconceivable without the Poor, without the intervention and the perpetual presence the poor, whose maintenance I solicit, in consequence, in the theater and in novels.

"A rich man, by contrast, cannot lay claim to any kind of bushel. His light is impossible to hide, since he is at home everywhere. He leaps to the eye; his identity oozes from his every pore, at least in literature. The whole world stares at him, and God himself is so embarrassed by the need to fabricate a role for him in his Mysteries that he has been obliged to abandon him to the hackneyed and negligible practices of beneficence.

"If, therefore, a massacre is necessary, and even quite urgent, I dare to open the proposal of a preliminary selection, a conclusive and irrefutable verification of individuals."

"The anthropometry of souls, then," specified the psychologist, who was determined to be irritating.

"I'll consent to that fashionable word, or any other that suits you—but in any case, it will require the sieve of God, for may the Devil take me away if anyone, here or elsewhere, has the ability to award himself a passport of any considerable value.

"No one knows his own name, no one knows his own face, because no one knows of what mysterious—perhaps worm-eaten—individual he is, in essence, taking the place."

"You're making fun of us, Apemantus," Madame du Fondement put in, then. "You promised us a story."

"You're determined, then—so be it.

"A rich man had two sons. The younger said to his father: 'Father, give me the share of your property that will come to me.' And the Father divided his wealth.

"A few days later, the younger son, having gathered up everything he had, departed for a distant region, and there squandered all his wealth in luxurious living. . . ."

"Oh," cried the young Baronne du Carcan d'Amour, for whom the fashion was invented of lowering necklines to slightly below the navel, impetuously, "but that's the parable of the prodigal son that the gentleman is telling us. He's going to tell us that his hero was reduced to herding swine and dying of hunger, and that one day, weary of that profession, he came back to his father's house, who felt very tender on seeing him come back from far away."

"Alas no, Madame," Apemantus replied, in a very grave voice. "It was the swine that came back. . . ."

The conversation was at that point when someone who did not have a pleasant smell came into the apartment.

A Cry from the Depths
(Extract from *The Poor Woman*)

To André Roullet[1]

Ne postituas filiam tuam,
ne contaminetur terra,
et impleatur piaculo.
Leviticus xix, 29.[2]

THE abode was sinister.
It was black Parisian poverty dolled up in its deception, the odious bric-à-brac of the former comfort
of bourgeois workers, slowly undone by dissipation and
burning desire.

Firstly, there was a large Napoleonic bed that might have
been beautiful in 1810 but whose brass had been stripped
of gilt since the Hundred Days; its varnish was gone, its
castors crippled, and even its legs were lamentably patched,
their countless scratches testifying to its decrepitude. That

---

1 A friend and correspondent of Bloy's, mentioned on numerous occasions in his journals, who does not seem to have been otherwise
distinguished.
2 The A.V. rendering of the verse reads: "Do not prostitute thy daughter, to cause her to be a whore; let the land fall to whoredom, and the
land become full of wickedness."

bed without delights, scantily garnished with an equivocal mattress and a pair of dirty curtains, inexpertly hidden beneath a gelatinous quilt, must have broken the backs of three generations of furniture-removers.

In the shadow of that monument, which took up a third of the mansard, another mattress was visible, spotted with lice and black with dirt, simply spread out on the floorboards.

On the other side, an old Voltaire armchair, which one might have thought had escaped from the sack of a town, was allowing its entrails of wrack and iron wire to emigrate, in spite of the almost amiable hypocrisy of a shred of infantile tapestry.

Next to that item of furniture, which all the second-hand dealers had refused to acquire, surmounted by its water-jug and bowl, was one of those minuscule tables from crapulous lodging-houses, which makes one think of the Last Judgment.

Finally, in front of the only window, there was another table, in walnut, devoid of luxury and equilibrium, which the most assiduous polishing could not have induced to shine, and three wicker chairs, two of which were almost caved-in.

The linen, what remained of it, ought have been packed in an old shaggy padlocked trunk on which visitors sometimes sat.

Such was the furniture, similar enough to many others in this joyous capital of binges and disarray—but what was unusual and atrocious was the pretention of proud dignity and distinction that the inhabitant of the place, Madame Demandon, had spread like a pomade over the mildew of that frightful hovel.

The hearth devoid of fire or ashes would have been melancholy, in spite of its hideousness, without the grotesque clutter of souvenirs and vile trinkets that overloaded the mantelpiece. There were little cylindrical globes protecting tiny bouquets of dried flowers; another little spherical globe mounted on a base of conchyliferous concrete, in which a spectator could see a Swiss landscape floating; an assortment of univalve mollusk shells in which a poetic ear could easily have perceived the distant murmur of waves; and two of those tender Florian shepherds, male and female, in colored porcelain, fired for the multitude in some unknown factory of ignominy.

Among these works of art were tucked devotional images—doves drinking from golden chalices, angels bearing armfuls of "the wheat of the elect," curly-haired first communicants holding candles in lacy paper—and two or three mundane questions, such as "where is the cat?" or "where is the gamekeeper?" inexplicably framed. Finally, there were photographs of workers, soldiers or shopkeepers—an incredible number of effigies, which rose up in a pyramid toward the ceiling.

Here and there, along the walls, in the intervals between tattered garments, hung a few frightful chromolithographs, purchased at fairs or delivered by clothing stores. The sentimental Demandon was very fond of such horrors. That simpering beggar-woman was one of the most discouraging incarnations of the idiotic vanity of women, and the decay of that "supernumerary bone," as Bossuet put it, would have caused the plague to recoil.

The mattress lying on the floor served as a bed for her daughter, who rejoiced in the ridiculous name of Cymodocée. The poor child had slept there during the two years that their black poverty had been acute. She slept there as a punishment for her resistance to the will of the old woman, who had tried in vain to maneuver her into lucrative business with well-off gentlemen.

Cymodocée Demandon belonged to the category of those sad and touching beings, the sight of whom enlivens the constancy of the tormented. She was pretty rather than beautiful, but her tall stature, slightly stooped in the shoulders by the weight of evil days, gave her a rather grandiose air. That was the only thing she got from her mother, to whom she was the angelic opposite, contrasting with her in infinite disparities.

Her magnificent hair, of the most striking black; her vast eyes, those of a captive gypsy, "from which darkness seemed to flow" but in which floated vanquished fleets of Resignation; the dolorous pallor of her childish face, whose lines, modified by exceedingly strict anguish, had become almost severe; and, finally, the voluptuous suppleness of her poses and her gait, had won her the reputation of possessing what the bourgeois gentlemen of Paris call, between themselves, "a Spanish look."

Poor Spaniard, singularly timid! Because of her smile, one could not look at her without wanting to weep. All the nostalgias of tenderness fluttered like desolate little birds frightened by a woodcutter around her lips, devoid of malice, which one might have thought vermilion-tinted by a paint-brush, so readily did the blood from her heart rush there for a kiss.

That heart-rending and divine smile, which begged for mercy and simply wanted to please, could not be forgotten when one had obtained the most banal kind attention therefrom.

She was scarcely twenty years old. Twenty years, already, of misery, trampling and despair! The bruised roses of her adolescence of penal servitude had been cruelly stripped of petals by storms, in the black bowl of the melancholy garden of dreams. Even so, an entire orient of youth was still deployed within her, like the luminous transudation of her soul, which nothing had been able to wither.

One sensed so clearly that a little happiness would have rendered her ravishing, and that, in default of terrestrial joy, the humble creature might perhaps have caught fire, like the amorous torch of the Gospel, on seeing Christ pass by with bare feet.

But the Savior, nailed so many centuries ago, does not descend from his cross expressly for poor girls, and the personal experience of the sad Cymodocée was incapable of fortifying her with the hope of consolation.

She scarcely slept that night. Her thoughts caused her too much suffering. She was cold, too, shivering under the threads of her rags, for winter was already beginning.

She thought, as she gazed into the darkness, that it was very cruel not even to have the right to weep in a miserable corner. Assuming that the horror of soiling her tears would not have prevented them from sometimes spreading over the dung-heap of that pig-sty, such a melancholy would have been instantly criticized by Madame Demandon as a proof of selfishness and criminal cowardice.

That old caterpillar of Purgatory had always rigorously forbidden complaints, saying that a child ought to be the recompense and the "crown" of a mother. She had even borrowed humid phrases on that subject from the ejaculatory rhetoric of the devotional images of which she was an idolater.

The unfortunate girl's heart, compressed in an implacable vice, had therefore silently resorbed her pain, without ever being able to barricade or harden itself.

Whatever might be done to her, she agonized in the thirst for love, and, having no one to cherish, she sometimes went into churches in the middle of the day, in order to sob there at her leisure in the depths of some utterly dark chapel. Those hours of emotional indulgence had been the best of her life, and the simulacrum of passion that came later certainly was not worth as much.

At least they had not unleashed bitterness, those blissful hours in which the wellsprings of her heart silently invoked the wellsprings of heaven.

She remembered having sensed Gentleness itself, and when she dissolved in tears, she had a very distant, infinitely mysterious impression, a kind of anonymous presentiment of having slaked unknown thirsts. . . .

One day—oh, the memory of it would never be effaced—a Personage had spoken to her, a priest with the long white beard of a patriarch, bearing the pectoral cross and the amethyst, who seemed to have come from those solitudes situated in the confines of the world in which the evangelical lions of the Episcopacy prowl under terrible skies.

Seeing such a young woman weeping, he had approached, considering her benevolently, He had blessed her, with a very slow benediction, moving his lips softly, and then placing his hand on her head in the fashion of a dominator of souls.

"My child," he had said, "why are you weeping?"

She could still hear that calm and penetrating voice,

which had appeared to her to be the voice of a superhuman being—but what could she have replied, at such a moment, if not that she was dying of the desire to live?

She had merely looked at him with her large eyes of a lost kid, where so much pain was legible.

It was then that the stranger had added these astonishing words, which she would never forget:

"Someone must once have talked to you about Eve, who is the mother of the human race. She is a great saint in the eyes of the Church, although she is scarcely honored in this Occident, where her name is often mingled with profane reflections—but she is still invoked by we Christians of the old Orient, where ancient traditions are conserved. Her name signifies the mother of the living. God, who knows all our thoughts, doubtless determined that I should remember her when I saw you. Address yourself, therefore, to that mother, who is closer to you than the one who engendered you. She alone, believe me, can help you, since you do not resemble anyone, poor child, who has a thirst for Life. Adieu, my gentle daughter; I'm leaving shortly for distant countries, from which I shall probably never return, because of my great age. When you are in pain, remember the old missionary who will pray for you in the depths of deserts."

And he did, in fact, leave, after having left a twenty-franc piece on the arm-rest of the prie-Dieu, to which she remained nailed by astonishment and the most indescribable respect.

Incapable of obtaining information on the spot, she knew nothing about that old man, whom she believed to have been sent expressly by the Father of suffering children. For her, he was simply "the Missionary."

The entire incident returned thus to her memory during the dolorous insomnia. She had been scarcely sixteen then, and since then, great God, what had she become?

She had not succeeded in understanding that frightful fall—for facts are inexorable. They know no pity, and oblivion itself, if one can obtain it, is impotent to annihilate their crushing testimony. . .

"All the power of Heaven can do nothing to prevent my belonging voluntarily to that man, and being soiled by him until death. O my God! Oh my God!"

Moaning, she had sat up in the darkness. She became mad with anguish when that idea reappeared to her with precision.

Her adventure had been one of heart-breaking banality. She had succumbed, like a hundred thousand others, to the irremovable trebuchet of the most vulgar seduction. She had ruined herself simply and stupidly, with a Faublas[1] of the ministry who had neither promised her nor given her anything, not even momentary pleasure, and from whom she had neither hoped for not expected anything.

The crucifying truth was that she had surrendered herself to some lady-killer because he had found her in his path, because it was raining, because she was sick at heart and in the fibers of her being, because she was weary of dying of the uniformity of her torments, and probably also out of curiosity. She no longer knew. It had become utterly incomprehensible to her.

And what odious platitude there was in that intrigue of busy shops and fixed-price restaurants! Her best excuse

---

1 The protagonist of *Les Amours du chevalier de Faublas* (1787) by the Revolutionary activist Jean-Baptiste Louvet de Couvrai, and its two sequels.

had been, perhaps—as always, alas!—the illusion easily procured in such an unhappy girl by a well-dressed man whose politeness seemed exquisite.

The liaison had lasted for some while, and by virtue of a nobility of heart, out of pride, in order not to be a prostitute, although it scarcely helped her, she had forced herself conscientiously to love that fellow, of whose egotism and pretentious mediocrity she was all too well aware.

But now, it was over. Nothing remained to her but an intolerable disgust for the wretched lover whose narrow soul she could have accepted, but whose astonishing cowardice had saturated her with all the flaws of scorn and aversion.

Betrayed, abandoned, outraged and boorishly pelted with ordure by the very man to whom she had sacrificed her unique flower—what a rigorous punishment for a single day of folly!

Now, therefore, what would become of her? Could she truly not escape the odious fate of which her mother had spoken?

The law of the unfortunate is, in truth, too harsh. Was it, therefore, impossible for a poor girl to escape prostitution in one manner or another?

What would the missionary say? What would he say, that fine old man who had so clearly seen that she was dying of a thirst for life? The memory of that unknown man, living or dead, made her weep silently in the darkness.

She was not, in her own judgment, any better than the most utterly ruined. Her sin having been committed without intoxication, nothing was capable of attenuating the bitterness and humiliation. That perpetual recurrence hypnotized her, immobilized her, made her seems stupid sometimes, with her panicked eyes of a Cassandra of repentance wide open and staring. . . .

She had given away irrevocably, for the duration of all eternities, her only wealth, the most precious treasure that a woman can possess, even if that woman were the Empress of the Milky Way. She had given that away, and why?

Now, the Three Persons could do whatever they wanted—erase creation, banish time and space, refashion the void, amalgamate all the infinities—and all that would change absolutely nothing of the fact that at one moment she had been a virgin and the next she had not. It was impossible to undo the metamorphosis.

"What can I offer, then?" she murmured. "In what way am I preferable to anyone else that men roll in the filth beneath their feet? When I was good, it seemed to me that I was looking after snow-white lambs on a mountain full of perfumes and nightingales. Although I was very unhappy, I felt that I had a fount of courage within me in order to defend the precious thing of which I was the depository and which the Lord will no longer find. Today, my spring is polluted, my beautiful limpid water turned to mud, and the most frightful beasts swarm therein. I, who could have become a saint as bright as daylight, to pray with the angels on the edge of the carpet of the heavens, no longer even have the right to be loved by an honest man who might be charitable enough to want me!"

At that moment, the young woman's thoughts congealed like the blood of the dead. Her mother, completely drunk, came in, groping, knocking things over, emitting blasphemies and filth, and finally fell down, groaning, like a dangerous sow.

Here goes! the young woman said to herself. *I'll go as far as that, since it's impossible to do otherwise. What does one shame more or less matter? I can't be any more scornful of myself than I am now. So, don't think about anything any longer, and try to go to sleep, poor little lost dog who can't blame anyone. Your destiny, you see, is to suffer. That's almost what the missionary said to me—my kind old missionary, who ought to have taken me with him into his deserts, and is probably weeping, as he gazes at me from the depths of his tomb!*

The Reading Room

To Pol Demade, Belgian Catholic[1]

Literature is indispensable.

"**B**UT God's thunder! When someone tells you that there's someone. . . ."

Orthodoxie Panard, who had been trying the door handle momentarily, took flight when she heard the redoubtable voice of her paternal uncle.

The reading room was so ludicrously fitted out that only a single individual could enjoy it at a time, and there were ten people in the house. There was Père Panard and Mère Panard; the four heirs Panard, Athanase, Héliodore, Démétrius and Orthodoxie; then Uncle Justinien, Aunt Plectrude and Aunt Roxelane; and finally, good old Palmyre. That made ten, in all. It was absurd.

And take note that all of them, except Palmyre herself, had or might have intellectual needs of the most imperious nature.

Whatever time it was, one was always sure of finding

---

1 Pol Demade (1863-1936) was a physician and writer, best known for his fantastic fiction, much of which was collected in *Contes inquiets* (1898).

someone there. Sometimes there was a queue at the door. It was enough to disgust the family.

It as impossible to make that skinflint Panard listen to reason. He was a former professor of Greek—a member of the Institut, if you please—who never washed his hands, as an economy measure, and who declaimed the imprecations of Hecuba, in the same text by Euripides, when anyone talked to him about constructing a second premises.

He had no lack of money, though, since the famous inheritance he had received from that translator of Philostratus, a wealthy landowner. However, the contemporary literature with which the Panards who had emerged from his loins primarily nourished themselves being devoid of interest for him, he claimed that the present arrangement was satisfactory and pretended not to hear the optative insinuations of his heirs.

The most intolerable of competitors was Uncle Justinien, a retired colonel of the gendarmerie, who never finished what he was doing in there. Once the animal had succeeded in introducing himself therein, supplications and tears were futile. It was necessary to wait until he had finished shuffling papers.

If that tanned sheepskin, that interminable fetid dotard, that broken-down supplier of the guillotine, had, at least, had elevated motives for prolonging his vacations that way, for lingering indefinitely in the precious cabinet for three or four hours a day . . . but no! That veteran of misfortune, whom the heavens obstinately refused to lay low, had always been incapable of reading anything but the descriptions of malefactors or arrest warrants.

"Divine bounty, what can you possibly be doing in there?" cried Aunt Plectrude, raising her two arid arms toward the stars—for he often got up in the middle of the night.

"I'm doing my correspondence," he replied, with the finesse of a gendarme who could not be caught napping.

With all that, Orthodoxie was more unhappy than anyone else. She was a young woman of an uncommon grace, who had literary ambitions and was taking bicycle lessons.

Her brother Athanase, who had already launched himself into Symbolism had introduced her to the head of the Romano-Spada School, whose Greek roots were exceptionally agreeable to old Panard, and had advised Romano to take rapid advantage of that welcome to insinuate his inseparable friend, the great Papadiamantopolis.

One day, the very legitimate suspicions of the professor had been sufficiently vanquished to permit the invitation of the nonpareil and supereminent Péritoine, who deigned to come unceremoniously, in all frankness, with his aureole of toil.

Finally, the table expanding, several Klephtes, in their turn, had received hospitality because of their love of Pindar.

It is true that such a surfeit of guests rendered the little place even more inaccessible, maliciously occupied more than ever by Justinien, who only emerged to utter irredeemable incongruities at table.

That circumstance cast a shadow over the scene and, I repeat, Orthodoxie suffered therefrom in her most delicate recesses. An amiable virgin who wanted nothing more than to open herself up! A charming flower that a breath would have caused to blossom! How easy it would have been for her, but for the avaricious stinginess of her father, to launch herself into the joyous society where so many worthy masters would have patronized her efficaciously!

Unfortunately, it would have been necessary to break audaciously with an old man full of prejudices, whom that influx of apostles had already disquieted, and who was talking about bidding farewell to Attica and the Peloponnese.

With anguish, she saw the time coming when she would be almost reduced, as before, to self-education.

Oh, if Panard had only consented to let her read the brilliant productions of psychologists or mages! But that was out of the question. All the new works that authors or publishers sent with dedications to the stern member of the Institut were immediately expedited to that derisory cabinet, where it was impossible to obtain half an hour to oneself.

And it goes without saying that it was the only resource. One could only seek education there. As for taking pamphlets away, it was necessary to banish the hope. The rage of the old pedagogue, who dug around everywhere, would have burst forth in a terrible manner if anyone had dared remove a single tome from that private library, of which he had the catalogue in his formidable memory. It was absolutely necessary to use them on the spot.

Now, Justinien abused the privilege scandalously. When he had consulted studies of mores or collections of poetry, the pages were in such a state that one had, with a groan, to renounce reading them after him. Even the dedications had disappeared.

The sentimental Orthodoxie was driven crazy by that, no longer being able to pick up the thread of stories, suddenly finding herself deprived of a decisive chapter that would doubtless have clarified them, forced, in spite of her inexperience to construct improbable episodes herself and conjecture impossible denouements.

Necessity, it is said, is the mother of invention. This true story will furnish the proof of it.

One day, a robust porter arrived bringing the complete works of the celebrated Russian novelist Borborygme, which had finally been translated.

For a long time, the young woman had dreamed of reading the emollient and philharmonic pages of that relaxed Muscovite, but it was all too easy to foresee that the precious mass in question would not escape the common destiny of lyrical or documentary papers with which the reading room was continually filled.

In order to avoid that catastrophe, there was not a minute to lose. Orthodoxie therefore went immediately to find Aunt Roxelane, who was also fond of literature and was certainly, after her, the most euphonic person in the family. She was, moreover, no less stingy than Panard, and the latter had an attentive consideration for the capital she possessed and manipulated with prudence. She alone escaped the maniac's inquisition and her threshold was respected.

In a matter of seconds the conspiracy was organized. The two women arranged for the great man to avoid the profanatory hands of the colonel of the gendarmerie, and Palmyre, corrupted with illusory promises, took the parcel into Roxelane's room.

There were a few fine days then, the aunt and the niece reading and weeping together.

Unfortunately, the vibrant Orthodoxie could not contain her enthusiasm sufficiently. Unintentionally, she let

Slavic ideas and metaphors slip, and Panard's suspicions were awakened one morning. The word "rouble" having been pronounced by the imprudent individual, who thought she was talking about money, he rose from the table like a man struck by a sudden flash of light and hastened to the cabinet,[1] arriving at the very moment that the eternal Justinien had just emerged from it.

He was then heard searching the archives energetically for a long time, while no one dared budge, the storm being so close.

He finally reappeared, pale and red, rather like some ill-extinguished firebrand on which the north wind had blown.

"Where are my Borborygmes?" he howled.

Aunt Plectrude, informed of the machination, tried to defect the cyclone on to Justinien, but, the latter having sworn by his cross and his boots that he was unjustly suspected, the veracity of the old gendarme could not be put in doubt.

Orthodoxie, in her turn, overwhelmed by fear, charged her brothers Athanase, Héliodore and Démétrius, who did not even know what the fuss was about, so obstinately that the discerning patriarch had no difficulty detecting their innocence.

The matter was serious, and the punishment was proportionate to the crime. It was necessary to restore the precious volumes, which incontinently went the same way as their predecessors, and the only one who profited was the triply odious uncle, that literature acting upon him

---

1 Although Panard evidently noticed that the word was of Russian origin, it is possible that he also found it suggestive of *roublard* [cunning or double-dealing], or perhaps *rouable* [fit to be broken on the wheel].

with so much force that he no longer emerged from his lair except at meal times.

However, Orthodoxie, whose dolor was heart-rending, succeeded in consoling herself. She even finished up understanding that such is the last judgment of all human papers, and that reading is generally done in that way in families where reason is predominant, and that tangible felicitations are more estimable than the deceptive lucubrations of a few dreamers. . . .

But what am I saying? Had she not discovered, above all, on that occasion, the profound verity of the axiom formulated by one of our poetesses, and which was henceforth a guiding light for her: Before speaking it's necessary to turn one's tongue seven times . . . in someone else's mouth.

No One's Perfect

To Camille Lemonnier[1]

ESCULAPE NUPTIAL, being assured that the old man had received a sufficient number of knife-thrusts and had certainly exhaled what is conventionally known as the last sigh, immediately thought about having some fun.

That judicious man estimated that the rope cannot always be taut, that it is wise to have an occasional breather, and that every effort is worthy of its reward.

He had been lucky enough to get his hands on a large sum. Happy with life and with a delicately perfumed conscience, he went hither and yon, under the chestnut-trees and plane-trees, respiring the odorous breath of the evening delightedly.

It was spring: not the equivocal and rheumatic spring of the equinox but the heady renewal of the beginning of June, when the enlaced Gemini recoil before Cancer.

---

1 Camille Lemonnier (1844-1913) was a member of the *Jeune Belgique* group of Symbolist writers in his youth, although he went on to become a significant Naturalist writer. In 1888 he was convicted of "offending public morals" in a story in *Gil Blas*, and was charged with similar offenses on three other occasions, but acquitted.

Esculape, inundated with suave impressions, his eyes moist with tears, felt like an apostle. He desired the happiness of the human species, the fraternity of ferocious beasts, the protection of the oppressed and the consolation of those who suffer. His heart, full of forgiveness, inclined toward the indigent. He spread into extended hands the abundant copper coins with which his pockets were encumbered.

He even went into a church and participated in the common prayer recited by a faithful flock. He adored God, telling Him that he loved his neighbor as himself. He gave thanks for the wealth he had received, recognizing that he had been extracted from the void. He asked that the darkness, ugliness and malice of sin might be lifted from him, made a scrupulous examination of his conscience, and discovered tenacious imperfections and persistent trifles within himself: impulses of vanity and impatience, distractions, omissions, reckless and uncharitable judgments, etc., but above all, idleness and negligence in the accomplishment of the duties of his estate.

He concluded with a resolution to be less fragile from now on, to implore the aid of heaven for the dying and travelers, to ask, when appropriate, to be protected by night, and, penetrated by these sentiments, ran all the way to the nearest brothel.

He was committed to honest pleasures; he was not one of those men who lend themselves easily to frivolous dissipations. He leaned more to the side of rigor and only forbade himself the difficulty of a ridiculous gravity.

He killed in order to live, because it was not a stupid trade. He could, like so many others, have been proud of the dangers of such a ticklish profession, but he preferred silence. Like convolvulus, the flowers of his soul only bloomed in the shade.

He killed in the home, politely, discreetly and as neatly as could be. It was, one can say, work well done.

He did not make promises that he was incapable of keeping. He did not make any promises at all—but his clients never complained.

As for venomous tongues, he had a remedy for them. *Do well and let others say what they will* was his motto. The suffrage of his conscience was enough for him.

A private man, above all, he was very rarely seen in cafés, and even the malevolent were forced to render him the justice that, outside of the bordello, he saw almost no one.

Within that hospitable dwelling he had fixed his spiritual affection upon a scantily-clad young woman who made the establishment prosper and whose precocity as a virtuoso denoted enthusiasm. Scarcely out of childhood, numerous salons had admired her already. The fortunate Esculape had the knack of making himself loved, and time appeared to suspend its flight while those two beings leaned toward one another over the mystical lake. The ravishing Loulou no longer wanted to know anything else as soon as her little Cucu arrived, and the latter was often constrained to bring her back to the professional sentiment of the art, when the old gentlemen became impatient.

In return, she gave him precious information.

Eventually, they invested considerable sums with discernment. Loulou spent almost nothing, air and light being almost sufficient for her everyday costume, which was always simple and perfectly tasteful. Already, they could glimpse the reward, the happy future that awaited them in the country, in some remote cottage beneath the lilac and roses, which they would buy one day, and the peaceful old age with which Providence rewards those who have battled bravely.

Yes, undoubtedly—but alas, who can tell how many human hopes are vain?

What followed is exceedingly dolorous.

One night, Eculape did not appear. The house suffered in consequence more than one can say. Poor Loulou, feverish at first, then agitated and finally haggard, ceased to delight. A Belgian notary, who had brought his clients' funds, received a resounding brace of slaps, which astonished the passers-by.

The scandal was enormous and discredit imminent, but she did not want to listen to anyone or anything. Her anxiety mounted to the point of delirium; she pushed scorn for the rules to the extent of opening a window that had remained closed since the previous fourteenth of July and calling for her Cucu, in a terrible voice, in the great nocturnal silence.

A few protestant pastors put to sea, not without having expressed their indignation, and, as soon as he following day, serious newspapers sadly began to prognosticate the end of the world.

Ought I to say it? Esculape was on a spree. Esculape had encountered a serpent.

As he was returning sagely to the love-nest he was accosted by a childhood friend that he had not seen for ten years and who succeeded in debauching him for the first time in his life.

I do not know what sophisms that deadly friend deployed in order to turn him away from the narrow path leading to heaven, but he got him so drunk that, toward dawn, the moaning Loulou's pie-eyed lover took a cab to go in search of a *Combat spirituel*[1] that he remembered having forgotten the previous evening at his mate's home, and which he judged indispensable to his interior progress.

The faithful companion of the night led him, as if by the hand, all the way to the dead man's room, where the commissaire of police was obligingly waiting for him.

And that is how a single slip ruined two careers.

No one's perfect.

---

1 *Les Douze regles pour le combat sprituel,* translated into French from the Latin of Pico della Mirandola, was a popular conduct guide for the pious.

"Let's Be Reasonable!"

To Édouard d'Arbourg

"WHY aren't you eating, father?" Suzanne asked, her eyes filling with tears. "For two days now you haven't touched a thing and you don't want to see anyone. You're not ill, though; you would have called the doctor. Have you some great chagrin, then, that you don't want to tell me about? I'm no longer a little girl, as you know full well, and I'd be very glad to console you."

The individual to whom this speech was addressed was none other than the famous Ambroise Chaumontel, whose affairs interested half the globe: the incomparable advocate whose eloquence could have disentangled the very filaments of chaos and petrified the darkness.

The Maître was about sixty, and did not hesitate to say so. He declared it to everyone, on any occasion, for it was his placid mania to aspire to the dignity of the patriarchs. A few venomous rivals had accused him of dyeing his hair white in order to seem more august in pleading for some orphan, but he maintained his soul far above the envy whose impotent darts expired at his feet.

The discouraging reputation that he had acquired in a quarter of a century at the bar, his great fortune and the

189

high renown of a name that several generations of loud-mouths had made illustrious, put insurmountable extents between himself and the vile multitude.

In sum, he enjoyed an entirely English kind of consideration that nothing seemed to be able to erode, and passed, doubtless with good reason, for a perhaps-unexciting but exceedingly precious example of professional integrity.

It is necessary to believe that, today, strange worries were obsessing him, for he did not reply to his daughter and became even more morose, fixing his large eyes, accustomed to dignified gazes, on some object whose image was painted in vain on his retina.

He cherished, after his fashion, the amiable child who had miraculously become a beautiful young woman, whose mother, buried ten years before, was rumored to have been carried off by an overwhelming attack of respect. People said that her husband had been, for the poor woman, something like Mount Sinai, and that she had ended up dying of it.

Suzanne, more fortunate, had succeeded in making herself almost loved. By virtue of the effect of internal movements difficult to explain, the supercilious and pinnacular Chaumontel had leaned toward his daughter. For her alone, it is true, the wood of his heart was flexible. He pushed condescension so far as to suffer her caresses, and to permit a few affectionate locutions, a few familiar words. . . .

Nevertheless, today, I repeat, nothing could get a grip on him. Chaumontel had climbed back on to his column.

Suzanne, renouncing lunch herself, came to put one of her arms around her father's neck and, in a voice that would have soothed a ferocious ape, begged him to speak.

"You wouldn't understand, my child," he said, finally, utterly austere. And, getting up from the table, like a man weary of carrying the world on his shoulders, he slowly withdrew, without adding a single traitorous word.

This is what had happened.

Two days before, Chaumontel had met Bardache.

All the old prowlers had known Bardache, the tall Agénor Bardache, who was so pretty in the last years of the Second Empire, when he made his debut.

In that distant era, his nickname in the Rue Marbeuf was "Parents' Tranquility." The fellow had a great success, which a few dotards remembered. Illustrious people entertained him, and proud generals, tanned by the African sun, offered him rare bouquets.

After the Commune, which he had ornamented, I believe, with a few stripes, he disappeared for several years into the depths of the nadir.

The sidewalks of the secret wood saw him again one day, but how much he had changed! Bearded now, jaundiced and dirty, he resembled an arid tree that had put forth overly long branches. His angular face, plastered with singular lividities, in spite of greasepaint and powder, was reminiscent of those effigies of Unforgiven Evil, of which the Middle Ages sculpted so many, beneath the feet of saints, in the obscure corners of basilicas.

For the imaginative, that phantom of mud had to have hands moist with the sweat of the dying, and he was conclusively labeled the Cadaver in the strange pseudonymic society that he frequented.

One exceedingly sinister particularity was that the joints of his skeleton cracked as he walked, as is said of Pierre le Cruel.[1]

Ostentatiously, however, as much as an abominable rascal can be, he admitted to a position as a business journalist, and was seeking a rich marriage.

Chaumontel, who was content with himself and had just shaken innumerable hands on the threshold of the Chambre, was preparing to get into his carriage when he was stopped by that skimmer of putrescence, who touched him on the shoulder in a familiar manner.

"Well, little Deponent Verb,[2] don't you recognize old friends any more?" said the Cadaver.

Choking, the advocate recoiled. "Who are you Monsieur? I don't know you."

"You don't recognize me, my dear? Have I changed so much? Let's get into your hearse first. I'll refresh your memory."

"Baptiste!" cried Chaumontel "Go fetch me a policeman right away!"

"Oh, be careful, little Deponent of my heart. If you make a fuss, I'll spill everything. I'll tell the commissaire of police about your youthful farces, the little house in Marly and the room of deep sighs where people amused themselves so much. I could even let him admire your

---

1 Pedro I, King of Castile from 1350 to1369, whose name was thoroughly blackened by the chronicler Pero López de Ayala, although his supporters preferred the nicknamed Pedro the Just. His alliance with the English during the Hundred Years' War won him a posthumous lament by Chaucer.

2 A deponent verb is one that is active in meaning but passive in voice. Bardache (whose name signifies his former status as a male prostitute) is accusing the lawyer of hypocritical self-representation in a manner that a trained Latinist would easily grasp.

photograph, which I always carry on me . . . you know, your photograph 'as a flower of the fields that one goes to pluck,' which you were so kind as to offer me, having had it taken just for me, and adding a suggestive dedication?"

At these words, Suzanne's father, having gone very pale, hurriedly recalled his coachman and, seeing that he was observed, pushed the frightful companion that destiny had sent him into the carriage himself. On a curt order, the horses departed at a rapid trot.

"Well, is it money you want?" he began.

"Money?" the other replied. "What do you take me for? I have the honor, Monsieur Chaumontel, of asking for your daughter's hand."

"My daughter's hand!" howled the renegade of Sodom, conscious of himself as a father. "My daughter's hand! Are you going to mingle my daughter's name with your filth now?"

"Come, come, my dear friend—calm down, if you please, and let's be reasonable. We're no longer children, are we? Nor even young men. The time for beautiful follies is past. I've lost all my advantages, I'm losing my plumage by the day, I'm bored to death and scarcely alive. I want to become honorable, like you, my dear friend. For that, I need money, undoubtedly, but I also need a wife. It's quite natural that I should cast my eyes on you, who can give me both. Mademoiselle Suzanne is quite simply delicious.

"Oh, don't bawl—it's absolutely futile. This is it: I have your captivating photograph, and I also possess a few no-less-precious letters with which you once honored me. Fair exchange is no robbery. You understand me. I'll give you a month to arrange the matter—six weeks at the most. Beyond that limit, I'll blow everything up. Personally, I've nothing to lose. Now, tell your coachman to stop. I'll get out here."

"One more thing," stammered the unfortunate, who had just rolled down ten thousand steps. "You've forgotten that I can kill myself."

The other, already on the footplate, burst out laughing. "I'm not afraid of that," he said, not without profundity.

Two months after that conversation, Agénor Bardache married Suzanne in a village in Normandy in which the advocate owned an old house.

No one was invited and the announcements, confided to Chaumontel's care, were thrown into the latrine.

This story is substantially true. I'll tell you on another occasion how the spouses died. The father is still alive, thank God!

Oh, I forgot—on the day of the marriage, when the ceremony was over, the radiant Bardache leaned toward his father-in-law and murmured, amorously: "Oh, my friend! How much she resembles you!"

Jocasta on the Sidewalk

To Ladislas Lubanski[1]

Sanctum nihil est ab inguine tutum.[2]
Juvenal, sat. III

MONSIEUR,
    When you receive this letter I shall certainly be on my way to Africa, where I shall attempt to kill myself in an honorable manner. If that can be called suicide, I think that the method is acceptable, even for a Catholic like you.

I'm weary of living, I agree—absolutely and irremediably fatigued by what imbeciles and swine, between themselves, call life.

Do me the honor of believing that my affairs are in order. I do not owe money to anyone, so no creditor will weep over me. The small income of which I made scarcely noble use will pass into pure hands when I am gone.

---

1 Colonel Jean-Clément-Ladislas Lubanski (1854-1906) used the pseudonym Jean Star to publish *Tonkinades* (1902) but published a guide to amateur astronomy under his own name.
2 The quotation from the third satire actually reads *Sanctum nihil est, et ab inguine tutum*. The approximate meaning is: "Nothing's sacred to them or safe from their pricks." The text proceeds "Not the lady of the house. . . ."

I have no family, and the group of my friends or ac-quaintances is hardly worth a memory. My disappearance will not even be noticed, even by a humble dog.

Before disappearing, however, I have decided to tell you a secret of frightful sadness and ignominy, the divulgation of which, I believe, might be useful to a few individuals.

It is understood that you are perfectly free to publish this anonymous confidence, unless you judge it, in your conscience, more expedient to destroy it.

When this confession has been written and put in the post, I shall become as complete a stranger as the unknown drama sleeping in the limbo of a novelist's imagination, and I have taken measures to ensure that no one will be able to recognize me.

Act, then, Monsieur, as you please. Here is the poem.

When I lost my mother at the age of six, I recall that my grief was extreme—much greater, I suppose, than befits a child of that age, for it caused me to harvest an unusual quantity of slaps.

I shall never be able to forget the piercing, the ripping of my little heart when I was informed, brutally, that I would not see her again, that it was all over for the lovely Mama, and that she had been buried in the earth amid the dead.

I could scarcely comprehend what it was to die, but I was pounded by terror, crushed by horror, and I have never been able to make a complete recovery.

I was not shown the corpse. There was a reason for that, which I only found out much later.

My cries were such, at any rate, that my father, a very hard man who detested me, sent me away that same day to the country, on the edge of a very somber fir-wood, in the vicinity of a fetid pond, not far from the establishment of a horse-slaughterer: a sinister place that I can still see.

I lived there for two years, entirely deprived of education, under the eyes of a withered peasant woman, who nourished me as meanly as possible and allowed me to roam around all day.

Poor little Mama, in the midst of the dead!

I often went to wander around the slaughterer's fence, drawn to it as if dragged by claws. I could not see very much through the planks, but I could breathe the abominable odor of the place and I often saw enormous rats filing in front of me: mysterious frightful creatures that appeared to come from the pond.

I came to think that perhaps it was there that they had put her, the dead woman—for I already had a presentiment that the world is made in the infamous image of that yard of killers of suffering beasts.

I must have moved God to pity when I came—how many times!—to throw myself against that enclosure and call out to my mother, sobbing.

Oh, I was completely abandoned, I assure you. My father, whom I scarcely saw once every three months, for an afternoon, regaled me exclusively with slaps, calling me a "young idiot," an "exalted cretin," and a "little thief," and having no hesitation in expressing, in polite terms, his desire to see me die before much longer.

I remember that one day, having talked about a walk, he led me along the bank of the pond to a muddy spot full of reeds, where I often stopped for hours on end to contemplate the swarming of tadpoles or newts. Suddenly, he ordered me harshly to go pick a water-lily for him that was floating a few meters away, and when I tried to obey that pitiless man, I felt with terror that I was sinking into the mud. When he pulled me out, blaspheming, I was shoulder-deep, and I'm convinced that, but for the presence of a witness attracted by my desperate screams, I would have stayed there, so diabolical was his expression.

Such was the vestibule of my existence. I expect that you've had enough of that debut, so I'll pass over the miserable years that followed—years in internment in a school in which my father had me locked up for ten years.

Believe me if you can: until the age of eighteen, I did not leave that prison for a single day.

For those whose childhood had a few joys, it will evidently be useless to try to make them understand what the effects might be of such a long and ferocious incarceration. It appears that the civil law permits such things; it is antique paternity, if I'm not mistaken.

Fortunately or unfortunately, I was sufficiently robust not to die of it—except that I don't know what became of my soul during that putrefaction. Ten years of contact with pupils and teachers would putrefy a bronze horse, as you know. A number of writers have demonstrated that superabundantly, and I don't think there's any need to insist.

Only one precious thing remained to me: a sort of exceedingly pure flower in a virgin corner of my ravaged garden. That was the infinitely sweet memory of my mother. A souvenir of delights, luminous and soothing! Having lost her so soon, I was unable to reconstitute the lines of her dear face, but I remembered having seen her as very beautiful, and the marvelous softness of her caresses was immortal.

The last time, especially, she had been so sad and so tender, my beloved mother, so tender and so profoundly sad, that when I thought about it, I felt myself melting with pity. . . .

I shall hasten to the denouement of the story, which is killing me, devouring me, soiling me worse than anything that can be imagined.

When I emerged from the school, the man who called himself my father had grown so old that I had difficulty recognizing him—but he had, I believe, become more atrocious.

His hated for me, although inexplicable, appeared to me to have been exasperated into a kind of chronic rage, difficult to describe, which made one think of demonic possession. The first few nights, I barricaded myself in my room, fearing that he would take advantage of my sleep to cut my throat: a childish fear, no doubt, but quite justified by certain glances that he darted at me slyly.

There were few or no words, however; our souls saw one another. One had the sensation of being face to face on the edge of a gulf. A few brief orders, a few harsh and cutting monosyllables—that was absolutely all.

I had no need of genius to divine that he had only brought me back in order to inflict some further torture upon me, but I was now a man. I had experience acquired in the ignoble tribulations of collegiate internment, and I would have defied a young lion to be better armed than I was.

How could I foresee the nameless thing, the ineffable horror, that the monster had reserved for me?

He was an architect charged with important projects, and I was immediately given into the petty care of a head clerk who was to initiate me in the art of building.

That individual, whom I studiously and very slowly exsanguinated last week, before leaving Paris, was a man my father trusted, his damned soul. I remembered having always seen him in the house. He made me work unrelentingly from morning until night.

The first month having been completed, he suddenly adopted a friendly manner to declare to me that his employer, less harsh that I appeared to believe, had decided to gratify me every month with a reasonable sum, although I would have no need of anything under his roof.

"But," he added, "everyone knows what young men are like. Pleasure is necessary to them after a day's work, and your father understands that completely. I've even been instructed to give you a key to the front door, in order that you can come in at any hour you please when you go out in the evening. No one wants you to feel that you're a prisoner."

The money that intermediary gave me—my first money!—naturally softened my heart and I no longer thought of mistrusting him.

He immediately took advantage of that by extracting all possible confidences—which was not exactly a Herculean labor, since I was eighteen years old and did not have a friend on earth.

Becoming increasingly friendly, he gradually became my chaperone in libertinage, deigned to get drunk in my company, and introduced me to the best places.

Let's skip to the final episode.

One day, the terrible fellow, who knew what he was doing, gave me the address, which he had doubtless held in reserve for the opportune moment, of a woman, "charming, although a trifle mature," who would heap me with delights.

Two hours later, I lay with my mother—who only recognized me the next day.

Yours sincerely, etc.

Cain's Lucky Find

To Henry Hornbostel[1]

I DON'T know how, toward the end of that memorable dinner, we reached such a degree of stupidity that we began talking about objects found on what is mysteriously and amphibiologically known as the public highway.

Almost everyone took advantage of it to recount adventures with recumbent treasures and bags tripped over that contained great riches—adventures of which, one was forced to agree, the lack of interest was striking. Some, less drunk, lowered their heads and confessed that they had never found anything.

It was then that, collecting all disseminated attention with a broad gesture, the loud-mouthed sculptor Pélopidas Gacourgnolle, addressed us.

"Do you know," he bellowed, "what Marchenoir's luckiest find was?"[2]

A collective nutation of heads revealed to him that no one knew anything at all about it.

---

1 Another of Bloy's correspondents—obviously not the American architect, but possibly the French economist still active in the 1930s.
2 Caïn Marchenoir is the protagonist of *Le Désespéré*, acknowledged by Bloy to be a self-portrait.

"Then, my children, listen to this. The anecdote is worth the trouble of being told.

✳

"It's common knowledge," he said, "that our literary Grand Inquisitor was once the most impregnable and calamitous adolescent who ever displayed our sidewalks the cataclysm of frock-coat and trousers. The luxuriance of that dreamer's vagabondage is indescribable.

"I remember having seen him many a time in that era, and I'm so proud of it that I have difficulty believing that the earth can support me. Oh, I could talk about it at length. I was not yet his friend, and had no inkling that I would be, one day. I don't even know whether he had ever had a single friend.

"He was a stormy and awkward young boar who only hung out with the constellations. One divined that he was impatient with any other promiscuity, and I don't believe that anyone every attempted the recruitment of the primitive.

"All of you know him too well for me to knock myself out painting a picture of him, but I don't know whether you can imagine him at eighteen, as a ferocious self-portrait painted in shark-oil represents him, which he only exhibits to his most intimate acquaintances. He appears there, biting a fist, in a mastic of bitumen, burnt umber and lead carbonate, fixing the spectator with two terrible eyes, bloodshot by force of intensity. Until you've seen that, you haven't seen anything. . . .

"That was the first affectation of our hero, who wanted to be a painter a long time before he sensed that he was a writer, and who would have been, believe me, in his painting, exactly what he is in his frightful books: the silky mastiff and the celestial cannibal we all admire.

"The eyes of that portrait, obsessive to the point of astonishing a virtuoso of my stamp, were never, it is true, those eyes of implausible softness that the creator of volcanoes and luminaries lit up in his morose face for the confusion of imbeciles. They were sufficient, nevertheless, to determine an extraordinary resemblance that the most audacious longevity will never be able to belie, because they are the eyes of his soul, the true eyes of his profound soul, eternally avid for divine presentiments.

"Evidently, when he executed that exorbitant effigy, his instinct, as one sequestered in the midst of gulfs, had already alerted him to his execrable destiny. Undoubtedly, he had caught a whiff of the carrion that would clutter his path and whose exhalations would almost asphyxiate the three hundred lions he had within him.

"How could he not have had a vision of that infernal future, which, one is compelled to assume, emerged from his gladiatorial faculties? For I don't know any other man whose nature was so clearly designed as his in black snakes and violent vexations.

"Unfortunates less privileged ought to bless him, since he was and still is the isolating lightning-conductor that soaks up all thunderstorms. The miracle was offered by him, twenty years ago, of a blasphemer of the rabble, absolutely invincible and always in his stirrups, in spite of the whirlwind of the crapulous and the cyclone of the pusillanimous.

"Oh, he can boast of having been unleashed, that one, and of having seen off proud gentlemen who called themselves his companions. The amities or simple admirations he encountered seem to me to resemble those divine matches that 'only catch fire on the box,' according to the formula with which the Septentrion has gratified us.[1]

"Heaven preserve me from an additional jeremiad on the agriculture of affections and the political economy of cordial cement. The man of whom I'm speaking has, in any case, expressed himself in such a definitive fashion that any rhetoric on this point will henceforth be idle. We all know the atrocious discomfort of not having been born in the skin of a dog when the destined irritant refused the groin of a fortunate pig. . . .

"Everyone will tell you that the famous indigent was frantically rescued by innumerable benefactors, and that the entrails of contemporary charity will probably never be healed of the tumors caused by his ingratitude—but it is in the literary world, above all, that he is said to have perpetrated depredation. There is no ultimately murky depth of the writing-desk that has not been gladly exploited, like a diamond-mine, by that crystalline legend, who has become akin to an intractable calculation in the bottommost layers of the secretions of journalism.

"I have cared for some of those exciting valetudinarians, whose complaints have been instantly refreshed by the soles of my boots. They remembered, then, never having really *known* the supposed parasite. Marchenoir has obtained those miraculous cures several times in person, and his methods, superior to mine, are so infallible that I hold him to be the most sublime oculist of memory—capable, I'm convinced, of operating on the cataract of Niagara!

---

1 "Safety matches" were invented by a Swede and commercially developed in the same country.

"But I'm getting carried away," Pélopidas said, sitting down again—for he had got up momentarily, and was marching back and forth, knocking things over. "I'm deprived all self-composure when I think of that animal, who would kill a superior man in order to glean three sous in the dung of the influential baboons of Primary Paris.

"I was telling you, then, that I had caught a glimpse of Marchenoir in the distant epoch of his novitiate in the odysseys of famine and grotesque disguise. I was myself, in those days, a vile enough poor wretch of a petty plasterer, who tested the weight of his torso against the horizontals of the quarter more often than he masticated the clay of the academy. I was quite a rake, one of those compartmentalized rogues who dramatizes nonsense, and would probably have played some dirty trick on the wretch that was seen passing from time to time in front of the studio, ecstatically deciphering a battered second-hand book that seemed to be a continuation of his own astonishing rags.

"But there was the instructive legend of a certain student of chalcography who had, one day, steeped himself from head to toe in a pool of mud without even interrupting his reading, and had then set about drying himself by swinging from the supports of a balustraded window that the sun was bombarding ardently—an episode that gave one to reflect.

"Then again, imbecile as I was, the grandiosity of that poverty had an effect on me. I sensed, even so, the presence of an extraordinary soul—and later, I came to understand that that was exactly what revolted the offspring of cockroaches infesting our epidermis every time the unusual wretch appeared.

"His rags, I assure you, had nothing ignoble about them. The propriety of his frayed second-hand clothes was, in fact, rather curious and touching. I can still recall a certain top hat acquired God only knows how long before, the absurdity of which could only have been surpassed by Thordvaldsen's unforgettable headgear in the fresco mocking the winds on the exterior wall of his museum in Copenhagen, a tribute of the decrepit admiration of the Danes.[1]

"That hat, familiar with all weathers, was seen to be transformed in the course of the seasons, passing through various colors. Its final observed condition was a spiraling Archimedean screw of white circumvolutions, which made the head appear to be coiffed by the stump of a column torn by the earthquake from some Portuguese basilica—a decisive phase followed, barely a month later, by an irremediable collapse of which three or four bumpkins from the studio were the bewildered witnesses. I could never describe the solicitude with which he polished that undefinable object.

"After the catastrophe, he went through the streets bare-headed.

"I don't believe that he was every literally bare-foot, but his boots would have been judged more ancient than the sandals of the most decrepit anchorite. I ask permission not to persist with this verse of my poem, which would end up being as long as *Paradise Lost* and would dry us out as much as the evangelical preambles to the end of the world if I lingered over the accessories.

"It would require I don't know what hyperbole to give a glimpse of the envelope of that aborigine of misfortune, who, at a distance of many years, I imagine as tailored by the very claw of the Angel of Humiliation.

1 The reference is to the Danish-Icelandic sculptor Bertel Thorvaldsen (1770-1844), whose museum is next to the Christiansborg Palace.

"And that's quite enough digression; I'll get back to my story.

"When I had the extreme joy, long hoped-for, of becoming the friend and companion of Marchenoir, I was the unfortunately impotent witness—I was not rich then—of the unspeakable insults that an old landlady made him endure.

"He was several months behind with the rent and could not succeed, whatever he did, in satisfying her. That filthy woman was always on at him, with all her might, to give her money. She kept him, nevertheless, but as one keeps pearl-bearing oysters in the fisheries of the Indian Ocean, continually watched by attentive sharks, having put the most rigorous embargo on the three-quarters-destroyed furniture that he had inherited from his mother and always on the lookout for any opportunity to strip him of the miserable windfalls that came his way.

"The unfortunate tenant was condemned to never leaving his room without enduring the fire of the demands of the ferocious sea-eagle, who insulted him several times a day in the presence of all the neighbors, and often abused him in the middle of the street.

"That situation had endured for ten years, Messieurs. Marchenoir had never succeeded in making up the arrears and could not resolve to take flight. For the sum of three or four hundred francs, that old shrew tortured him for forty seasons.

"Don't get impatient, please, I'm getting to the anecdote, but what you've just heard was necessary to enable you to sense the unique importance of the find he made, that 'beautiful swallow of such a sweet summer' at the delightful hour when the convolvulus and crowfoot of the woods open their flowers.

"It was already three years since the compassion of the Oceanides had succeeded in unchaining our Prometheus. A first literary success, discounted by inexpressible torments, had permitted him finally to cut the cable of ignominy and he was living tranquilly in a solitary quarter, infinitely far from the horrible jail. The image of the female vulture had gradually blurred and dimmed, becoming indiscernible and telescopic. It was impossible to recover the print, even in the most profound latrines of his memory.

"One day in July, shortly before dawn, the sunrise having scarcely been advertised, Marchenoir went out, as was his custom, to refresh himself on the bastions and read a few pages of Saxo Grammaticus or Perotto's *Cornucopia*.

"Having taken sixty paces or thereabouts, as he looked at his feet in order to turn the corner of his street, he perceived a short distance away, in a deserted area where nothing existed then but the enclosures of market gardens and wasteland, a bureaucratic box of the most notarial or official form, whose presence astonished him.

Approaching close enough to touch it with his foot, the resistance of the object redoubled his astonishment, which immediately turned to fear when he saw a trickle of blood.

When the lid was rapidly flipped back, his landlady appeared to him: the severed head of his former landlady, gazing at him with her dead eyes, her dead white eyes that resembled two large silver coins.

The Animal-Lover
(Extract from *The Poor Woman*)

To the Friend who arrives unexpectedly.

*Eratque cum bestiis, et angeli minsitrabant illi
Mark, chapter I.*[1]

"I DON'T KNOW," the Comforter said to us, "if the word *story* is precisely suited to what you're about to hear. It's more a memory of a voyage, an old impression, which has become very vivid and very profound, that I'd like to share with you.

"It happened on the mount of La Salette, where, as Catholics are aware, the Virgin appeared in 1846 to two poor children.

"Naturally, everything possible has been done to dishonor that prodigious event by ridicule and calumny, but what does that matter?

"So, I found myself in that place of pilgrimage and, on the very first evening, I had come energetically to the

---

1 *Mark* 1:13. In the A.V. the entire verse reads: "[And he was there in the wilderness forty days, tempted by Satan:] and was with the wild beasts, and the angels ministered to him."

defense of a stranger, one of my companions at the host's table, whom all the guests were showering freely with their hypocritical sarcasms. I had even forced one of those brutes, among whom there were two or three ecclesiastics, to beg his pardon.

"You know that it is in not my nature to tolerate the weak being oppressed in my presence. My client was an individual with a sad expression, dressed like a country-dweller, whose simplicity had attracted my sympathy. He was being mocked because he was a sort of vegetarian, not admitting the killing of animals and forbidding himself to eat their flesh under any pretext whatsoever. He said as much to anyone who cared to listen, without any per-siflage being able to restrain him, and one sensed that he would have given his life for that idea.

"The following day, the first person I saw beside the miraculous spring was my protégé. He was praying, totally absorbed, and I was able to observe him.

"He was a man of vulgar appearance, dressed in an al-most wretched fashion. He must have been over fifty, and was already showing the marks of an imminent decrepi-tude. One divined that all the storms of misfortune had descended upon him. His timid and sickly face would have been insignificant, I think, but for an expression of singu-lar joy that appeared to be the effect of an internal con-versation. I saw his lips moving feebly, sometimes smiling in the pale and gentle fashion of a few idiots or thinking individuals whose soul is immersed in a gulf of spiritual affection.

"His eyes, above all, astonished me. Fixed on the bronze image of the Lamenting Virgin, they were speaking as two mouths might have spoken, like an entire population of supplicant or laudatory mouths! I imagined, on the divine register where the vibrations of hearts will one day be transposed in sonorous waves, an entire carillon of praise, amorous divagations, thanks and desires.

"It even seemed to me—and I retained that impression for years—that in the midst of the surrounding mountains, then girdled by blinding mists, a thousand threads of light, of an infinite softness and tenuousness, came to settle on the calamitous face of that worshiper, around which I believed I could see vague effluvia floating. . . .

"When he had finished, he came toward me and took off his hat. 'Monsieur,' he said, 'I would be glad to talk to you for a moment. Would you do me the honor of accompanying me on a short walk?'

"We went to sit down behind the church, on the edge of the plateau facing the Obiou, whose snowy summit the sun, still invisible in the mists, splashed at that moment.

"'You caused me a great deal of pain yesterday evening,' he commenced. 'I couldn't stop you, unfortunately, and I'm very sorry about that. You don't know me. I'm not an individual to defend. Once, when I didn't yet know myself, I defended myself, all alone. I was a hero. I killed a friend in a duel, over a joke.

"'Yes, Monsieur, I killed a being formed in the image of God, who had not even offended me. And that is called an affair of honor! I struck him full in the breast, and he died gazing at me, without saying a word. That gaze has not quit me for twenty-five years, and as I'm speaking to you now, it is up there, before me, on that old column of the firmament. . . .

"'When I imagine that moment, I'm capable of enduring anything. My only consolation and my only hope is that people mock me, insult me, shove my face into the dirt. Those who do so, I love; I bless them with all the benedictions of the world below, because that, you see, is justice: the true Justice.

"'You became angry and forcefully abused a man whose boots I am certainly not worthy to lick. You forced me to pray for him all night, lying at the threshold of his door, like a corpse, and this morning I begged him, by the Five Wounds of Our Savior, to tread on my face. . . .

"'Oh, Monsieur, don't try to justify me, I implore you. Say nothing humane to me. I ask you that, for the Love of God, who has walked upon this mountain. Believe me, everything that might color an infamy, I have said to myself, and may others have said it to me as well, since the hour when it was given to me to understand that I was the most ignoble of murderers.

"'The man that I killed had a wife and two children. The woman died of grief, do you hear? I have a million for the orphans. If I did not give everything I had, it was because family interests, stronger than I am, were opposed to it. But I have promised to live, until my final hour, in the fashion of a mendicant. I hoped thus that peace might return to me, as if the life of a man could be paid for in money. It is the money of prices and priests that I have given to those poor children, treated as little Judases by their father's murderer. Oh, yes indeed! It has never returned, that divine peace, and I am crucified every day!

"'I am telling you this, Monsieur, because you have taken pity on me, and might have conceived some esteem for me. I am still too cowardly to tell my life story to everyone, as I doubtless ought to do, and as the great penitents of the Middle Ages did. I tried to become a Trappist, then a

Chartreux. I was told everywhere that I had no vocation. Then I got married in order to glut myself with suffering. I married an old prostitute of the lowest rank, whom the sailors no longer wanted. She showered me with blows and soaked me in ridicule and ignominy. . . .

"'I let her want for nothing, but I put the debris of my fortune, which was still considerable, in a safe place. It is the wealth of the poor, from which I take a few small sums for my travels. Last year I was in the Holy Land, then at Compostela. Today, I'm at La Salette for the thirtieth time. People must know me. It's here that I've received the greatest help, and I urge all the unfortunate to make this pilgrimage. It's the Sinai of Penitence, the Paradise of Dolor, and those who don't understand it have much to mourn. Personally, I'm beginning to comprehend, and sometimes, I obtain release for an hour. . . .'

"He stopped, but I refrained from breaking his train of thought. I would, in any case, have been incapable of saying anything that would not have seemed ridiculous in the present of that voluntary convict, that colossal Stylite of Expiation.

"When he began to speak again, a few moments later, I was surprised by an unexpected transformation. Instead of the formidable pathos that had just squeezed every fiber of my heart, instead of that swell of remorse, that volcano of lamentation hurling the lava of anguish in all directions, there was the humble and mysteriously placid voice that I had heard the previous evening.

"If I ask you to imagine, for example, a dying child that you could hear speaking through a wall, it would be absurd—and yet, I can find nothing better. In brief, I had the intuition of something infinitely rare.

"'People often mock me,' said that voice, 'with regard to animals. You have witnessed that. I believe I can divine in you an imaginative man. You will be able to suspect, therefore—supposing a reckless zeal on my part—that I have given myself to that ridicule for the sake of pleasure. Not at all. I really am made like that. I love animals, of whatever sort, almost as much as it is possible or permissible to love humans.

"'I have sometimes desired, I confess, to be a total imbecile, in order to escape the sophisms of pride entirely, but that desire not having been realized thus far, I do not know what might occasion scorn for that manner of feeling, which extends, in me, as far as passion and which very sage persons have reproved.

"'Is there not a misunderstanding here? Can it be that the majority of people have forgotten that, being creatures themselves, they do not have the right to scorn the other aspects of creation? Saint Francis of Assisi, whom even atheists admire, considered himself the near relative, not merely of animals but of stones and spring-water, and the just Job was not criticized for saying to putrefaction: you are my family.

"'I know that God has given us the beasts as nourishment, but he did not give us a commandment to devour them in the material sense, and experiments in the ascetic life, over tens of centuries, have proved that human strength does not reside in that aliment. Universal Love in unknown because people do not see the reality beneath appearances. . . .'

"He spoke to me like that for a long time, with a great faith, a great love and, I beg you to believe, a marvelous divination of Christian Symbolism that I was very far from expecting of him. I owe a great deal to that simple man, who gave me, in a few conversations, the luminous key to an unknown world.

"I assure you that he was prodigious when he talked about animals. No more of the great heart-rending outbursts of his first confidence, no more tempests, no more dolorous meteors: a divine calm, and what candor!

"Placidly, he lit up like a tiny lamp set in a dwelling guarded by angels. As I listened to him, I remembered the fortunate individuals who were the first companions of the Seraphic One, whose hands full of flowers have perfumed the Occident, and I also saw again all the other saints of yore, whose pitiful feet have left us a few grains of the sand of the heavens.

"The little that I have told you about his words should have enabled you to glimpse that it was not a matter of those imbecilic transports that are perhaps the most disgusting mode of idolatry. Animals were, for him, the alphabetical signs of Ecstasy. He read in them—like the elect that I have mentioned—the only story that interested him: the eternal story of the Trinity, which he spelled out for me in the symbolic characters of Nature.

"My delight was inexpressible. In his eyes, the empire of the world, lost by the first Disobedience, could only be reconquered by the full restitution of the devastated ancient order. 'The animals,' he said to me, 'are, in our hands, the hostages of the vanquished celestial Beauty.' Strange words, whose profundity I have not yet measured. Precisely because the Beasts are what humans have most misunderstood and oppressed, he thought that one day God would make something unimaginable of them when the moment came to manifest His Glory.

"That is why his tenderness for those creatures was accompanied by a sort of mystical reverence, difficult to characterize in words. He saw in them the unconscious possessors of a sublime Secret, which humankind had lost beneath the foliage of Eden, and which their sad eyes, covered in darkness, can no longer divulge, since the frightful Prevarication. . . .'"

The Comforter said no more. Leaning his elbows on the table and pressing his temples with his fingertips, in one of his familiar poses, he gazed vaguely ahead of him, as if he were searching in the distance for some great bird of prey, desperate to avoid capture, which reflected his melancholy. . . .

"What became of the man?" one of us asked.

"Oh! Yes, my story isn't complete. I never saw him again, and I learned that he had died, a year later, from one of my compatriots resident in the little town in Brittany where he lived, by the sea.

"He died in the most terrible fashion, and, in consequence, the one he most desired—which is to say, at home, under the eyes of the abominable Xantippe whom he had chosen expressly to torture him.

"Struck by paralysis shortly after our encounter, he did not want to be transported to any sanitarium where he might have been at risk of dying peacefully. Having lived as a penitent, he wanted to die and yield his last breath as a penitent.

"It appears that his wife left him to lie in his own faeces. The details are frightful. It was even thought, briefly, that she had poisoned him. It is certain that she must have been impatient for him to die, hoping to inherit from him—but precautions had been taken long before, as he had told me, and the remains of his patrimony have gone into the hands of the poor. The lease of that cook of his agony expired naturally with him.

217

"Now, my story is entirely finished. You can see that it isn't very complicated. I simply wanted to enable you to see, to the extent that I have been able to see him myself—incompletely, alas—an entirely unique human being, of which, I am convinced, no other exemplar exists in the entire world.

"Without the exceedingly precise letter of my Breton correspondent, I would sometimes be tempted to wonder whether all of it was real, whether that encounter was anything but a mirage of my brain, a kind of interior refraction of the Miracle of La Salette, which was thus modified in passing through my soul.

"The poor man has remained there, like a parabolic analogy of that gigantic Christianity of old, which our abortive generations no longer want. For me, he represents the supernatural combination of the infantilism in Love and depth in Sacrifice that was the whole intelligence of the first Christians, around whom roared the hurricane of the dolors of a God.

"Mocked by imbeciles and hypocrites, a voluntary indigent and sad until death, when he looks at himself, betrothed to all torments and the satisfied companion of all opprobrium, that passionate of the Cross is, in my eyes, the exceedingly faithful image and miniature of those defunct times when the earth was like a great vessel in the gulfs of Paradise.

OTHER SNUGGLY BOOKS YOU WILL ENJOY ...

BLUE ON BLUE
by Quentin S. Crisp

A SUITE IN FOUR WINDOWS
by David Rix

NIGHTMARES OF AN ETHER-DRINKER
by Jean Lorrain

DIVORCE PROCEDURES FOR
THE HAIRDRESSERS OF A METALLIC AND
INCONSTANT GODDESS
by Justin Isis

BUTTERFLY DREAM
by Kristine Ong Muslim

GONE FISHING WITH SAMY ROSENSTOCK
by Toadhouse

METROPHILIAS
by Brendan Connell

THE SOUL-DRINKER
AND OTHER DECADENT FANTASIES
by Jean Lorrain

Lightning Source UK Ltd.
Milton Keynes UK
UKOW03f2217300117

293220UK00005B/467/P

9 781943 813155